REVELATION

WRAK-AYYA: THE AGE OF SHADOWS
BOOK SIX

LEIGH ROBERTS

D0556923

DRAGON WINGS PRESS

Editing by Joy Sephton http://www.justemagine.biz
Cover design by Cherie Fox http://www.cheriefox.com

Sexual activities or events in this book are intended for adults.

ISBN: 978-1-951528-09-6 (ebook)
ISBN: 978-1-951528-12-6 (paperback)

To all the children in the world, who find solace and hope
in the quiet hours, wondering...

What If?

CONTENTS

CHAPTER 1

In the meadow, where they would soon go their separate ways, Haan was ready to show the High Protector how to make the Locust tree break. The place was ringed with these trees—trees with a hard wood that took a long time to decay and were, therefore, a favorite of the People.

"When making the tree break to contact us, always use a Locust tree. The height of the break, the direction of the break, the twist—all are important."

Akar'Tor, still sulking from having to leave Kthama, stood by and watched silently. Khon'Tor had only recently discovered that Akar'Tor was his son, the product of the volatile relationship with his first mate, Hakani, whom they believed had jumped to her death decades ago, taking the unborn offspring with her.

Haan looked at Acaraho, sizing up his strength and height. He reached over and grabbed a Locust tree, and at about Acaraho's chest height, easily snapped it backward, the break exposed. Then he twisted the broken portion.

"That break means that this is a place of meeting —a point along a traveled path. For you, this additional part—" and Haan pulled the twisted portion so that it peeled the bark partway down the trunk, "— signifies a request for contact. This is only for the Akassa."

Akassa. Adia said that is what they call us, Acaraho remembered. He nodded.

"Now, you do the same." Haan pointed to a tree next to the one he had broken.

Acaraho made the same break, though it took more effort on his part.

"Always two together, broken in the same direction. Then twist and peel. It means you want to contact us, and we will come to you."

Acaraho nodded. *Khon'Tor will be glad to know we can now at least try to contact them.* He shivered as a sudden chill ran up his spine and the hair stood up on the back of his neck. A rustling from across the clearing caught his attention.

As if from nowhere, with hardly a sound, five other Sarnonn appeared, standing shoulder to shoulder.

Acaraho instinctively froze. If one Sarnonn was intimidating, a group of them standing this close was nearly paralyzing. He stood speechless, his eyes locked on an impenetrable wall of power.

Slowly, one of the smaller in the group broke away and started walking toward them. Acaraho clenched his teeth and held his place.

Hakani and Akar'Tor stepped away from Haan and walked toward the approaching Sarnonn. As they came together, Hakani pulled the wrap away from the offspring and held her up for the other to see. The Sarnonn put her arm around Hakani and made what looked to be a sign for congratulations, and then a flurry of female chatter broke the stillness.

Acaraho relaxed a bit upon seeing the welcoming behavior. He could not make out the chatter between the females, but it had a familiar motherly quality. The other four kept their place, apparently waiting for Haan's lead, and he tried not to stare. *This must be a bit what it is like for Ogima Adoeete's people when I enter the Brothers' village. I wonder what they thought of Nadiwani staying with them these past few weeks? I wonder if the novelty wore off after a while?*

Then Acaraho snapped his attention back to the moment. *I am losing my edge,* he warned himself. *They may be under Haan's control, or they may not be; when you make assumptions, you put yourself in danger. I know better; I must stay focused.*

Haan motioned to the other four to approach. Acaraho stood his ground, though his body was well into fight or flight response. *They are so big. Alone, none of us would stand a chance against one of them.*

The four approaching were not quite as tall as

Haan. Massive shoulders spanning more than the length of one of Acaraho's arms, large heads on thick necks, and the same thick coat of body hair everywhere. Despite his self-control, Acaraho shuddered.

One had darker hair coverings than the others, but aside from that, he could not tell them apart. In the sunlight, all their coats had that greenish undertone he had noticed before. He had never seen anything like it on any other animal.

Acaraho corrected himself. *They are not animals. They are people, just like us. Only somewhere, generations before, some of them bred with the Brothers to become us.*

Haan pointed to Acaraho and spoke to the Sarnonn. "This is the Akassa's High Protector, Acaraho." He then stepped over to Acaraho and offered his palm. Fortunately, Khon'Tor had told Acaraho about this gesture of goodwill. Acaraho placed his own palm on Haan's and drew it back toward himself. He flipped his palm over so Haan could do the same. It was a signal of friendship, safety, and welcome. The four giants dropped their shoulders and flexed their hands, yet still seemed to exude tension.

That is odd. What possible threat could I be to them?

Hakani and the fifth Sarnonn, whom Acaraho now knew to be a female, joined the group of males. Haan addressed them, again pointing to Acaraho.

"Acaraho is the High Protector at Kthama," he repeated. They all nodded.

Acaraho's eyebrows shot up. *How do they all know about Kthama?*

"Kthama?" He repeated.

The five nodded. "Kthama, your home," the female replied. "Ages ago, it was our home. But it belongs to you, the Akassa, now."

Haan nodded, then turned to Acaraho. "Did you never wonder why Kthama is so—" Haan made the Handspeak sign for massive or huge. "Kthama was the Mothoc's home first."

Acaraho was not sure he was following. *Who were the Mothoc? Did this group not call themselves the Sassen?*

Acaraho pointed to himself and said, "I am Akassa," then pointed to all of them in the circle and asked, "You call yourselves Sassen?"

They nodded.

"Who are the Mothoc?" he asked.

Haan stepped away and picked up a stick. He kicked away the ground cover, making a bare spot in the soil. Then he smoothed it with his foot and drew on it with the stick.

Acaraho shook his head and exhaled. *Is it possible they know far more about the Wrak-Wavara than we do?* Acaraho took a breath and stepped out on a limb. "Wrak-Wavara," he said. *The Age of Darkness.*

The five looked over at Haan. Haan repeated, nodding, "Wrak-Wavara."

Acaraho knew about Wrak-Wavara from attending the last High Council meeting. It was the dark period of the People's past, the details which had mostly been lost over the ages and were kept alive only by re-telling over time, down through successive High Council members.

"How do you know about Wrak-Wavara?" Acaraho asked.

"We were there. The Sassen remember."

"Yes, but it was long, long ago."

"Not so very long ago. The parents of my parents were part of the exodus from Kthama."

His parents' parents left Kthama? How could that be? My people have lived there for multiple generations. Just how long do the Sarnonn live?

Haan scuffed out what he had drawn in the dirt and ended the conversation, "We will go. I need to get my mate and offling home."

Acaraho held out his palm and they made the parting gesture. He watched them walk away, the hair on the back of his head standing up again. Haan's Handspeak was rudimentary, and his manual dexterity not at the level of the People's. But, as Oh'Dar had discovered, combining Handspeak with verbal language helped considerably, and Acaraho was confident he understood what Haan had told him.

I have to get back and tell Khon'Tor.

It was dark by the time Acaraho made it back to Kthama after accompanying Haan and his family through the valley. He went directly to Khon'Tor's quarters.

"Did you only return now, Acaraho?" asked Khon'Tor, sitting up slowly as the High Protector entered. The Leader shook his head to clear it and rubbed his eyes, still fighting the sickness. "What part of the day is it?"

Kweeuu, the wolf, raised his head and flopped his tail against the stone floor upon hearing Khon'Tor's voice.

"It is just past twilight. I am sorry to wake you, but I have important information you must hear now. We have to make sure the High Council meeting takes place as hoped."

"I do not understand. Did Haan show you how to make the special tree break to summon him?"

"Yes. And just after he showed me, five Sarnonn appeared out of nowhere."

Khon'Tor was now wide awake. "What do you mean, *out of nowhere*?"

Khon'Tor propped himself up further. "And why do you say that the High Council meeting must take place? We have already agreed it *should*."

"Yes, I know. Since you are awake now, let me tell you what Haan shared."

"Wait, where is Tehya?" asked Khon'Tor, looking around for his mate after realizing that her spot on the bed was empty.

"She is visiting Adia. She is safe. I passed them on the way in."

Khon'Tor nodded. "Continue, then."

"First of all, Haan did show me how to make the tree break so we can connect with them again. I will show you whenever you are able to go outside. Haan had five others waiting for him in the valley. One was a female; she was very interested in Hakani's offspring. The other four were males. They deferred to Haan, following his lead the whole time. Oh'Dar's idea of combining Handspeak and talking worked very well. I am certain I did not misunderstand. But we have it all wrong."

"We have *what* wrong?"

"From what we heard at the High Council meeting, we believe that the Sarnonn bred with the Brothers to produce the People. But it seems that is not exactly right."

Acaraho set down three stones he had brought in. He set one on the ground and said, "Mothoc." Then he set the other two stones below that one but on the same line, creating a triangle. Pointing to one, he said, "the People," then to the other, "the Sarnonn."

Khon'Tor raised his eyebrows. "So, Haan said that the Mothoc are the ones from whom our two tribes split? You are right; that is not how we understand it. Our stories say that the Sarnonn mated with the Brothers, not that there was a common root further back. If this is true, I wonder what happened to them. If they were the original People, did they all die off?"

"I do not know. And if Haan knows, he did not say. He was forthcoming with some information, but I sensed he was not telling everything."

"So the Sarnonn have more of the story of Wrak-Wavara than we do," Khon'Tor said. "Or at least a different one."

"Yes, and there is more. Perhaps part of the reason they know more is that they might be unusually long-lived. Far longer than we are. Haan said that the parents of his parents lived at Kthama and if he meant that literally— Then the Sarnonn lived here either before us, or maybe *with* us—"

Khon'Tor let out a low, slow breath.

"So their stories are not passing down through as many generations as ours. Now I understand the urgency of the High Council meeting. We must bring this information to them. Is there more?"

"I am sure of it," replied Acaraho. "We may need to make contact with Haan again before the meeting."

Khon'Tor nodded. "Good work." He sighed. "I need to rest now. Please find Tehya and send her to me."

Acaraho could not stop thinking about what Haan had told him. *The Sarnonn have longer lifespans than the People. We live longer than the Waschini and the Brothers, but not as long as the Sarnonn. We probably lost some of that trait in breeding with the Brothers, just as we lost other attributes such as their full-body hair and thicker features. And if there was a root further back—the Mothoc—how long were their lifespans? And are there any of them still alive, somewhere?*

Oh'Dar had decided. It was time to return to Shadow Ridge. He had been gone far longer than he had expected, and his grandmother would be very worried by now. Still, he could not have left Kthama sooner, with so many of the People sick and his mother needing his help.

He picked up his traveling clothes—those he had made years ago before he first left Kthama and had recently altered to fit for this visit home, the design obscure so it would not tie him to the Brothers.

Kweeuu, the grey wolf he had raised from a cub, had tracked him down to his grandmother's home at Shadow Ridge. It was that which had brought him back to Kthama. Not knowing if it was an omen for him to return or simply that the wolf was missing his Master, Oh'Dar had brought Kweeuu back to Kthama for fear that he might be shot. And it had proven important that he come back. But now, it was important he leave.

He shook out the clothes, memories of his first

long journey to Shadow Ridge coming to life as he handled the buckskin. *Great Spirit, please let Grandmother and Jenkins and Mrs. Thomas be safe. Please let them all be there when I get back.*

Oh'Dar found his Waschini clothes and the Waschini boots he hated and lined them up with the rest of his supplies for the trip back. Since Kweeuu would be staying here, he would not need to carry as much. But it was still cold out, and he would not be able to supplement his food supply with blossoms and sprouts as he had on his first journey.

Adia entered his workshop to say good night. Oh'Dar looked up to see his mother's smile fade as she realized what he was doing.

"You are leaving."

"Yes, Mama. I am. I am sorry. I was just going to come and tell you."

"When are you leaving?"

"Tomorrow afternoon, if the weather holds up. I need to make sure Storm is ready to travel, and there are a few more things I need to gather." He went over and hugged her. He was still frail compared to her, but no longer skinny. He was tall enough that she could rest her head on his shoulder if she leaned over a bit. He felt her tears on his neck and savored the familiar smell of rose and lavender.

"I will be back, Mama. It is not forever. I still do not know where I truly belong, but this will always be home. And I will not stay away as long this time, I promise."

Adia nodded.

"I wish there was some way we could communicate," he said. "But there is no way to get a message here; it would be too dangerous."

Adia realized that she could make a Connection with Oh'Dar, but she doubted she could keep it light enough to prevent him from learning that Khon'Tor was Nootau's father. They had grown up believing that Acaraho had sired Adia's son, Nootau. None of them knew that the great Khon'Tor had taken Adia as a maiden Without Her Consent and had seeded her.

Urilla Wuti is still here. Perhaps she can help me with it, as she did with Nimida and Nootau when they were mere newborns.

"Promise me you will not leave before first light tomorrow?" she asked, now needing time to consult Urilla Wuti about this possibility. "Do not forget, you still have to say your goodbyes."

"I promise. I will also stop to see Nadiwani, Is'Taqa, and Honovi on the way back to Shadow Ridge, so if you have any messages for them, let me know."

Back at Shadow Ridge, Mrs. Morgan sat in her usual spot, sipping her morning tea, holding the oval locket she'd given her daughter-in-law as a wedding present.

It opened to reveal two etchings—one of her son, Grayson Stone Morgan II, and the other of his wife. Mrs. Morgan's other son, Louis, and his wife, Charlotte, had arranged their murder and that of the infant son and would spend the rest of their lives imprisoned for it. By some stroke of providence, though unknown to her for many years, the child had survived the slaughter. But where he'd lived before he showed up alive and well several years ago was still a mystery.

Where are you, Grayson? Are you alright? When will you come back? She set the locket on the table beside her, letting the fine silver chain drizzle over the top of it.

"It's too quiet here without you. And Miss Blain, your first teacher, has written asking for news of you," she said out loud, as if he were present in the room. Sometimes she did that. It was comforting, even though she knew he couldn't hear her.

When Acaraho found them, Adia was sitting in the eating area with Nadiwani and Tehya, accompanied by Tehya's assigned guard. Acaraho dismissed the guard for the moment, and straddled the bench, next to his mate. Seeing the leftovers of their meal, he realized he had not eaten all day.

Adia said, "Acaraho, Oh'Dar is leaving tomorrow."

"I am sorry, Adia. I know you are sad. Did he say when he would return?"

"No, but he promised he would. He is worried about his family back there."

Acaraho nodded. He turned to Tehya. "Tehya, when you are done here, Khon'Tor would like you to go directly back to your quarters with your guard."

"I will take him some food. I was hoping he would rest while I was not there. How does he seem?"

"I do not think the worst of it has hit him yet, and now Nootau has it too," Adia said.

Acaraho was silent. *If Khon'Tor is left sterile as a result of the sickness—as it seems many of our males may have been—there will be no offspring to take his leadership. He will not claim Nootau, and Akar'Tor is not suited. I am sure this is weighing on Khon'Tor's mind.*

"Have you just now returned from taking Haan part of the way back home? And Hakani and Akar'-Tor?" asked Adia.

"Yes, but I have been speaking with Khon'Tor about what I learned. We will have much to talk about at the High Council meeting." Acaraho glanced at Tehya, whom he assumed was not privy to the history of the Wrak-Wavara.

The High Council had agreed that both Healers and Healers' Helpers would be invited to the next High Council meeting. The members would need all the help they could get figuring things out, and all the Healers would have to be involved on an ongoing basis considering the severity of what the People were now facing.

"We need to start preparing in earnest for the meeting. At least it will not be as large a group as the one we hosted for the Ashwea Awhidi."

Tehya rose to leave, "I am tired. I am going to head back." Acaraho raised his hand, and the guard returned to escort her back to her quarters.

"Is the guard still necessary?" asked Tehya.

"Probably not, since Haan, Hakani, and Akar'Tor have left. But for now, I feel better knowing you are not alone. And so does your mate, since at the moment he is too sick to keep up with your whereabouts," Acaraho said.

The guard accompanied Tehya down the corridor to the Leader's Quarters, but not before she had picked out some food she hoped Khon'Tor would eat.

"We should get some rest too, Adia," Acaraho said.

Adia nodded, closing her eyes, trying to block out the fact that Oh'Dar would be leaving shortly.

☾

The next morning, Adia went to her mentor. "Urilla Wuti, Oh'Dar is leaving this afternoon, and I need your help. Before Nimida left, you made a Connection to her, so I would at least know she was safe. Can you do that for me with Oh'Dar? Though I certainly do not want him to experience anything of what Khon'Tor did to me."

Urilla Wuti nodded. "Yes, and since Oh'Dar is an adult, I can make it a little stronger. As you know, I had to make the most rudimentary Connection with Nootau and Nimida, because offspring cannot handle adult experiences. I will still create something less intense than a full Connection, though."

"Thank you, Urilla Wuti. Oh'Dar and I will see you sometime today. What are your plans?"

"I want to spend time with Nootau. Perhaps even Nimida."

Adia did not question her motives; she trusted Urilla Wuti totally. "Afterward, I want to hear what you think about those two. I am getting worried about how close they are becoming."

"The time is coming, Adia; I know I keep bringing this up. I am sorry, but like it or not, soon you are going to have to tell them they are brother and sister. Do not wait too long."

Adia nodded. She knew the longer she delayed, the greater was the risk of them becoming romantically involved with each other. *I am not helping them by being dishonest. But I am also not prepared to lose them by telling them the truth. Great Mother, give me strength.*

Later that morning, Urilla Wuti sat across from Adia and Oh'Dar.

"Your mother has asked me to open a channel between you and her, so you can each know the other is safe. This is an ability only a handful of Healers have and is not known outside a small circle. By sharing the fact that this exists, we are placing great trust in you.

"Though Healers have a greater seventh sense, all the People have the ability to sense on some level. Of course, we do not know whether this ability exists in the Waschini, and we will find out in just a moment. What I am going to establish between you and your mother will not let her read your mind, and she will not know the details of what you are doing—only that you are safe. And you will know the same about her. Is that acceptable to you?"

Urilla Wuti was mindful that he was a young male and probably did not want his mother to know his intimate thoughts.

Oh'Dar nodded his consent. "How will that happen?"

"I will handle all of it. All I need you to do is close your eyes and relax. And trust me."

Urilla Wuti reached for one of Oh'Dar's hands and one of Adia's. All three closed their eyes. It was nothing like a Connection, which was a sacred joining of souls. It was only a stirring up, an enhancement of what all living creatures already had the potential to experience.

A small current snaked between Adia's consciousness and Oh'Dar's. She could feel his health, his vitality. She could feel his sadness over leaving. That was as far as it went, but it was enough.

Urilla Wuti broke the Connection and turned to Oh'Dar. "What did you experience?"

Oh'Dar looked at Adia. "I could feel you, Mama. I could feel your sorrow about my leaving. But I could also feel that you were otherwise fine. I am sorry I am making you sad."

"Good," Urilla Wuti said. "From now on, you will each know the basics of the other's state of mind. You can call it at will, but if anything cataclysmic happens, you will know immediately without having to search for the information. I hope this is what you wanted, Adia. Sometimes it is best not to know."

Adia frowned at the warning. *Is there something bad coming that Urilla Wuti knows about? I wish she had not said that.*

"Mama, I will be going this afternoon. I have already said goodbye to everyone else. Will you and Father see me off?"

"Of course, son."

Then Oh'Dar had a thought. "Urilla Wuti, could you tell Kweeuu to stay here and guard Tehya? And that I will be back?"

Urilla Wuti laughed. "I think I can, Oh'Dar. I will make sure to do it before you leave."

"Thank you! It will give me much peace of mind if you can do that."

"If you wish, I can do better. Every living creature on earth has a connection with creation. Some are just more aware of it than others. Enhancing your own innate natural abilities, I can create a light stirring between you and him, so you can at least get an impression of how he is doing—and perhaps even more."

"Really?" laughed Oh'Dar.

Urilla Wuti smiled and nodded. "You might be able to develop this on your own if you sit still and practice it. All I am doing is giving your already innate ability a little boost. On second thought, bring Kweeuu to me. We can do it right now."

Oh'Dar went out and returned shortly with Kweeuu. The wolf sniffed at Urilla Wuti, then sat next to her without Oh'Dar's command.

"Are you ready?" asked the Healer.

Oh'Dar nodded. Urilla Wuti took his right hand and placed the other on Kweeuu's chest. He could feel something opening, but there was a different sensation than with his mother.

"It worked. I can feel him! It was more obscure, like looking through fog, like an impression or gut feeling, but it was there."

"Now you can tell him yourself that he is to stay and not try to find you again," Urilla Wuti said.

Oh'Dar sighed, greatly relieved. "Thank you, Urilla Wuti—and Mama."

He turned to Kweeuu and focused on creating an impression—that he was leaving Kthama and that Kweeuu would have to stay. Before Oh'Dar broke the stirring, he gave the huge grey wolf a command, "*Protect Tehya.*"

It was time. Adia prepared to say goodbye to Oh'Dar. She went to her quarters and found what she wanted, then went to meet Acaraho at the Great Entrance.

Storm appeared to be in great health. Oh'Dar had made sure to find time to exercise and groom the stallion during their stay, and his coat shone in the sunlight that streamed through the entrance. Oh'Dar set the packed saddlebags in place on the horse's back. He had changed back into his homemade clothing, which would be far more comfortable for the trip than his Waschini attire.

He turned to Adia, wrapped his arms around her, and squeezed her tight. Then he held her away from him, to meet her eyes.

"Mama, I will be back. And now, thanks to Urilla Wuti, you will know I am alright."

Adia nodded, then took something in both her hands and placed it around Oh'Dar's neck.

He looked down. It was the red jasper necklace he had made for her before he left the last time.

"Now you have to come back," she said. "This brought me more comfort than I can tell you. It was too precious to wear. But when you bring it back, I promise I will start wearing it. I am sure Tehya will be happy for me to follow her lead." Adia smiled, picturing the amber and amethyst necklace Oh'Dar had made for Tehya at Khon'Tor's request. Then she was serious again. "And when you come back, I will also tell you a story about why it meant even more than just being a beautiful and thoughtful gift."

Oh'Dar hugged Acaraho, then mounted Storm. "I will be back. I promise." He turned the stallion and left Kthama in the direction of the Brothers' village.

CHAPTER 2

It was still late afternoon when Oh'Dar reached the village. As he rode in, Is'Taqa's son, Nashoba, ran to greet him. Oh'Dar pulled Storm to a stop.

"Hello, Oh'Dar, you came back," observed Nashoba, reaching up to pet the stallion's neck.

"Yes, I did. Is your father around?"

Just as Oh'Dar asked, Honovi and Acise came out of their shelter. Nadiwani remained inside, used to staying out of sight, but then, hearing Oh'Dar's voice, she poked her head out and waved hello. He waved back, glad to see the beloved face of his honorary aunt.

"He is out with the braves," explained Noshoba, proud that Oh'Dar had asked him. "They are out hunting today."

"I am sorry I missed him. I stopped here to say

goodbye. Please tell him that I will be back and will make sure to see him then."

Nashoba nodded importantly. "Yes, Oh'Dar, I will tell him."

Oh'Dar could feel Acise's eyes boring into him while he spoke with her young brother. He dismounted and walked over to hug Honovi. "Thank you for all your help at Kthama. It does not look like you picked up the illness. Is anyone sick here?"

"So far, no. I am not sure why not, but I am grateful," Honovi replied.

Oh'Dar turned to Acise, who was patiently waiting for her turn to talk to him. Not knowing what he should tell her, he ended up being straightforward. "I will be back, but I do not know when. Please do not wait for me. I do not think I am the best match for you, and I do not want you to put your life on hold waiting for something that might never happen."

Acise threw her arms around his neck and hugged him. She whispered, "I love you, Oh'Dar. I always have and always will."

Oh'Dar unhooked her arms from his neck and gazed at her. Acise's eyes filled with tears. "I am sorry," he said, placing his hand against her face, not unaffected by her beautiful eyes and inviting lips.

He looked at her mother, Honovi, who nodded.

Then he mounted Storm and turned the stallion toward his grandmother's ranch.

"Tell Is'Taqa I said farewell!" he called out.

So Oh'Dar left the Brothers, and as soon as their home was behind him, he became Grayson Stone Morgan III once again, riding off toward Shadow Ridge.

☾

Oh'Dar traveled faster without Kweeuu. He did not have to worry about stopping for the wolf to hunt, nor be as concerned about staying hidden. Though he was not dressed as a Waschini, a horse and rider alone would not bring as much attention as a horse and rider with a grey wolf running beside them.

It was nearly a week before Oh'Dar reached the town where Mrs. Webb had taken him in. He made a special mark on his travel Keeping Stone before continuing on to Shadow Ridge.

☾

Jenkins looked up on hearing the distant pounding of hooves. He set aside the shovel and went out to look down the long driveway. "Well, for Heaven's sake. Look who's back," he said to no one in particular. "Vivian is going to be so happy." He started down the drive to meet Grayson Stone Morgan III.

"Master Grayson!" Jenkins called out. Oh'Dar pulled Storm up next to the Stable Master and dismounted. He grabbed Jenkins in a bear hug. "I told you I'd return on the back. "If I didn't know better, I'd think you grew another inch."

"I don't know; maybe I did! Where is Grandmother? And how are the two of you doing?" asked Oh'Dar with a wink.

"We're doing just fine, thank you. Your grandmother and I have been spending a great deal of time together since you left. Grayson, your timing couldn't be better. I'm going to ask Vivian to marry me. With your blessing, of course."

Oh'Dar clapped Jenkins on the back, "I'm very happy to hear that, Jenkins. Of course you have my blessing. You haven't asked her yet?"

"No. I keep trying to, but I lose my nerve. What if she says no?" said Jenkins sheepishly.

"Oh, I don't think she'll turn you down. I think you've both had your eyes on each other for some time now," grinned Oh'Dar.

"Let's go up to the house. Storm can wait a few minutes. Your grandmother's going to be so happy to see you, and if she thought I was keeping you to myself, I'd never hear the end of it."

Oh'Dar pulled off his saddlebags and started carrying them toward the house. Jenkins walked Storm into a stall, caught up with Oh'Dar, and the two men strode up the long flight of stairs together. Mrs. Thomas met them at the door, drying her hands on a cotton towel. Her eyes lit up when she saw Oh'Dar, but she put a finger to her lips.

"Sssh!"

Mrs. Thomas led them inside to where Mrs. Morgan was sitting, working on some cross-stitching.

"Ahhmm," Jenkins cleared his throat. Mrs. Morgan looked up from her needlework.

"Grayson!" She practically threw the embroidery aside and flew over to hug her grandson. Oh'Dar let the saddlebags slide to the floor so he could embrace her in return.

"Oh, Grayson. You're back. You're back!"

"I told you I'd come back. I'm sorry; I didn't intend to stay away so long, but it couldn't be helped."

"It doesn't matter. You're here now." She hugged him close. "Are you back for good?"

He sighed. *Why does everyone keep asking me that? I just keep hurting them all with my coming and going.*

"I'm back for now. I can't promise, Grandmother. I'm sorry. My life is—complicated."

Mrs. Morgan nodded, then walked back to the little table where she'd been sitting. She came back, holding up the little locket on its chain. "You wouldn't believe how many times I've held this, Grayson. I know you left it as a promise that you'd return. Thank you for that."

"I did. So, what have I missed around here?" he asked, changing the tender subject.

"Lots of new foals. Dreamer is doing his job. We have never had such fine colts and fillies. Wait until you see them," Jenkins said.

"Well, let me get out of these traveling clothes, and I'll be right with you. Is that alright, Grandmother?"

"Of course. Just be cleaned up and dressed in time for dinner."

Mrs. Thomas smiled. "I'll make something special for you, Grayson, and before dinner you can have a nice long soak in the tub—how does that sound?"

"That sounds perfect, Mrs. Thomas. Thank you so much. Jenkins, I'll be right out to take care of Storm."

Jenkins nodded at Oh'Dar, then smiled at Miss Vivian and gave her a wink before he went back to the barn.

Oh'Dar was glad to see his old room. He knew Mrs. Thomas would be busy all day now, refreshing it. He set his travel bags down by the bed and bounced up and down on the plush Waschini mattress. *We could learn a thing or two from the Waschini, that's for sure.*

Oh'Dar glanced over and noticed a letter on the side table. He picked it up and let out a long breath. It was from Miss Blain.

Oh'Dar ripped open the envelope. "*Master Grayson, I hope this letter finds you well. Mr. Carter wrote to me that you made excellent progress under his tutelage and were one of his best students. I'll be coming to Shadow Ridge for a visit this summer. I look forward to hearing how your medical studies are going. Yours very sincerely, Miss Blain.*"

Oh'Dar set the letter back down on the table. *So she's coming here for a visit. She thought enough of me to write. But she signed it Miss Blain, not Josephine. Jenkins said he thought I was taller. Perhaps now she'll see I'm a man and no longer the boy who was her student.*

Oh'Dar changed his clothes and met up with Jenkins in the barn. They talked as the stable master carefully brushed Storm down.

"So, when are you going to ask Grandmother?"

"Now that you're here, perhaps tonight. We could tie the knot this summer."

"Tie the knot?" Oh'Dar repeated.

"Get married. I don't think she cares about long engagements, being a widow for so long. Your grandfather died so many years ago. I wish you could have known him, Grayson. He and I worked so well together. I was just a farmhand when he hired me. He taught me all about horse breeding; if it wasn't for him, I would never have been prepared to take over and run Shadow Ridge when he died. Funny how things work out."

"I can't wait to see the look on her face."

Mr. Jenkins stopped and pulled out a pouch. He handed it to Grayson. Oh'Dar emptied it into his hand. A simple gold band slid onto his palm.

"Mrs. Thomas knows. I had her borrow one of Vivian's other rings so I could get the right size."

"Jenkins, I'm so happy for you both."

Oh'Dar enjoyed his warm bath, reflecting on the day's events, and thinking about Miss Blain.

He was ready for dinner on time. Mrs. Morgan was at her place at the head of the table, Jenkins was seated at her left, and Oh'Dar was back in his usual place on her right. Candlelight reflections danced on the wallpaper. Oh'Dar smiled, remembering how confusing it had been when he first arrived; walls, chairs, curtains all seemed to be covered in busy patterns. After the grey stone of Kthama, it had been a lot to get used to.

Jenkins took Mrs. Morgan's hand, and she took Oh'Dar's, and Jenkins said a blessing over their dinner.

I forgot to tell my family about this. They aren't all soulless monsters. They have some belief in the Great Spirit because they ask for a blessing over their food. How could I forget to tell them that?

"Mrs. Thomas, this is delicious. Thank you," Oh'Dar said as the housekeeper entered with another course. She patted him on the shoulder. Oh'Dar looked over at Jenkins, who was pushing his food around on the plate instead of eating. *He's nervous.*

"Grayson, I want to ask you about your visit back to—wherever—but I don't want to pry."

"It's alright, Grandmother. My visit went fine. I got Kweeuu back safely and believe he'll stay put now. I got to see the—important people I needed to see."

"You can return to your studies at the hospital now?" she asked.

Oh'Dar paused. *Do I want to, though?* he asked himself. "I'm not sure. I thought I might ask Dr. Miller if he'd take me on as a helper here, instead. That way, I wouldn't have to leave you again so soon."

"Do you still want to be a doctor?"

"Oh, yes. I reconfirmed that while I was gone. And Jenkins, I'd like to improve my sharpshooting skills and to learn about horse breeding, if you don't mind."

Jenkins looked up, "I didn't know you were interested in that."

"Well, it *is* the family business." Oh'Dar winked at him.

Mrs. Thomas cleared the plates, leaving the others seated at the table. Oh'Dar stared at Jenkins, a twinkle in his eye. Jenkins swallowed hard, then got up and stood beside Miss Vivian. She set down her tea and looked up at him as he stood by her side, not saying a word.

"Ben, what are you doing?" she giggled.

Jenkins pulled the pouch out of his pocket and took one of her hands in his. "Vivian, I'm trying to ask for your hand in marriage, but not doing so well at it, I'm afraid."

He spilled the ring out of the pouch into her palm.

She looked at the gold band, smiled, and stood up to embrace him. "What took you so long?" she teased, and gave him a kiss.

Oh'Dar turned to smile at Mrs. Thomas, who was watching from the doorway. "I'd say that the answer is yes, Jenkins!" Oh'Dar went over to congratulate them.

The next morning, word spread through the ranch that there would be a wedding soon. The farmhands and household staff wore big smiles for days thereafter.

Spring was well underway. Adia walked through the valley, breathing deeply in the fresh air. The rich soil smelled of rebirth. Birds filled the skies with song. She swept her hand over the budding leaves of the brush. *I wonder what Oh'Dar is doing this morning. I know he is safe, and he is looking forward to something. I will have to thank Urilla Wuti again for this Connection. It has taken a great burden off my mind—at least one of them.*

Adia's thoughts turned to Nootau and Nimida. Nootau was still sick with the illness that had ravaged their community. Khon'Tor was slowly recovering, and they now believed they had seen the last of it. *Nimida has hardly left her brother's side since he got sick. I have to tell them. I cannot put it off any longer. Great Mother, please make an opportunity and give me the words to say.*

Adia's thoughts were interrupted by a feeling that she was being watched. She had never felt that before in the valley. She stood a moment, listening, feeling. There was definitely *someone* out there. There was fear, but it was not her own. Hearing nothing, she turned quickly and started the journey back to Kthama.

Preparation was well underway for the return of the High Council members, the Healers, and their Helpers, people from all over the Sasquatch community. Acaraho was relieved; the more key people involved in the discussion, the better the chance that creative solutions would be found.

He sat at a table etched with a floor plan of Kthama's first level. Moving around a collection of small stones, he made plans for new accommodations.

Khon'Tor walked in, more slowly than usual, interrupting Acaraho's thoughts. "I keep returning to what Haan told you about the Mothoc. Could there be any left anywhere?"

"It is possible. We did not even know there was a community of Sarnonn living in our region. Considering the size of Haan's people, if the

Mothoc are even larger than them, I rather hope not."

"I am considering asking Haan to come and address the High Council."

Acaraho looked up from his accommodation planning. "If so, I suggest you make the tree break signals soon. There is no telling how long it will take for them to be found. We cannot assume the Sarnonn regularly monitor that valley. Of course, we cannot assume they do not, either. When they stepped out of the brush, it was as if they appeared from nowhere."

"I will go this afternoon."

"If you prefer, I will go. It is a bit of a walk for you, Khon'Tor, so soon after your illness."

Surprisingly, Khon'Tor nodded. "Very well."

That afternoon, Acaraho did as promised. He walked farther than the point where he and the Sarnonn had parted, wanting to make it clear that these were not the same breaks Haan had made during his demonstration. He selected two similar Locusts that stood next to each other, and made the breaks, twisting, then peeling a piece of bark down the trunk. The cracking of the Locust trunks broke the stillness. He stopped and listened. *Here I am already listening for a sign from them, but I have just told Khon'Tor it will take a while.* He shook his head and started back to Kthama. Part of the way, he noticed footprints in the softened earth. *Who was here ahead of me,* he wondered.

Back at Kthama, Acaraho took some time to chat with Adia.

"I took a nice walk in the valley this morning," Adia said.

"Did you? I was there this afternoon. I saw tracks coming back; they must have been yours."

"Probably. At least, I did not see anyone else out there. There were no tracks on my way out, but I did have a strange experience. I felt like I was being watched. I had to turn around and come back."

"Adia, I wish you would not go out there alone, especially not out that way. It is where Haan and I parted. I do not know that anyone is out there, but still—"

"I will not do it again. I hate to have a guard around, but you are right. We do not know how far away their home is. And Hakani is still not over her anger with us. Did you feel like that when you were out there? That someone else was there?"

"Not today," Acaraho said. "I had that feeling before, though, when I was there with Haan, just before the other five Sarnonn stepped out from nowhere."

"I know they are peaceful—I did not get any feeling that I was in danger—"

Acaraho interrupted her. "We *believe* they are peaceful. But we do not know that for a fact, Adia. I am learning how much we do not know yet, so let us not make assumptions about how peaceful they are or are not."

"Yes. You are right."

"Khon'Tor is considering asking Haan to attend the High Council meeting. That is why I went to the valley to make the signal for them to contact us.

"If he comes, will you interpret?"

"I will be glad to if need be. It is easy for me to understand him since I made the Connection. But I would rather he first try speaking, combined with Handspeak, to see if everyone can follow him."

Acaraho pushed his food around. "How is Nootau? I need to go and visit him."

"He is still sick. We can go together if you wish. Nimida has hardly left his side. I am afraid it is time."

He sighed. "On top of everything else going on—"

Haan and his traveling party made it back to their home safely. Hakani was greeted by the other females, who were interested in seeing the offling. Haaka was the first to ask to hold her, having been friends with Hakani from the beginning. She took the tiny bundle and Hakani bit her lip as she watched the little form in the arms of the hulking Sarnonn. *Even after all these years, I am still not used to living with them. They have been good to me, but Kayerm will never feel like home.*

As Hakani waited anxiously for Haaka to pass the offling back to her, she looked around the huge cavern. Similar to Kthama in many ways, Kayerm had the same high ceilings, but without the Mother Stream running through it, the ever-present dripping moisture was absent. The floors had been worn down to rock ages ago, and because of its sheltered opening, there was little fresh air coming in.

Life was harder here than at Kthama. Haan's tribe was not as organized as the People. There was more daily toil; with no Mother Stream running through the caves, they had to haul water daily from the Great River. There was no organized communal help, and the community was less cohesive.

The Sarnonn grouped into small pods within the larger community. Haan's pod consisted of himself, Hakani, Akar'Tor, and another two females. Both had become Hakani's friends—Haaka and Sastak. They were under Haan's protection as Leader, until such time as they should choose a mate—or someone should choose them. If they took a mate, the male would join Haan's pod. It was also possible that Haan would take one of them as an additional mate to Hakani. The females in Haan's pod, as well as others in the community, had helped Hakani recover from her strange journey there, and learn the way of life at Kayerm. She had been seen as Haan's first mate since Kesta died.

Hakani took her offling and went to their living area, a smaller cave down one of the tunnels off the back of the main cavern. She sat down on a large collection of grass and leaves and let the offling nurse. *I should never have gone back. I miss Kthama, and it is colder here than I remembered. I am getting tired of the daily struggle, and now I have this offling to care for. Maybe it would have been better if I had died when she was born. I know Haaka and Sastak will help me, but all we do here is survive.*"

Hakani moved the fur wrap away from her tiny offling's face and brushed the hair back off her forehead. *You definitely look more like us than them.* The down on her body was heavier than the People's, but not anywhere as dense or long as the Sarnonn's. Her nose was a little wider. The tiny creature wrapped her fingers around one of Hakani's. They were also a little thicker than those of the People's offspring. *Definitely a blend, but not as bad as I feared.* Hakani could not help herself; she had never been able to find the Sarnonn attractive. The best life she could hope for, for her daughter's future, would be to pair her with one of the People so she could live at Kthama.

Akar'Tor came in, pulling back the skin curtain in the doorway. He sat down next to Hakani and peeked at his new sister. "What are you going to name her, Mama?" he asked.

"I do not know yet. I have to wait and see."

"Are you glad to be back home?"

Hakani sighed. "No, I am not, Akar. I miss living at Kthama. It is hard to explain. Everything is harder here."

"But you were not happy there, Mama. You told

us Khon'Tor was mean to you. I have overheard you telling Father about it many times, and you spoke of it again while we were there."

"I know. I just wish there was a way to go back. And I wish I could let go of my anger over my life there. But when I think about him with *her*—"

Akar'Tor sat quietly, waiting for his mother to finish her thought. *I think she means Khon'Tor and Tehya. Why does she not like Tehya? Tehya is beautiful. Khon'Tor is lucky to have her. Maybe that is it. Maybe Mama thinks Khon'Tor should not have her because of what he did when she was his mate. What he also did to the Healer. None of this is fair. Mama is right, even though he is my father, Khon'Tor does not deserve to be Leader. We should be living at Kthama instead of him. And I do not know why, so long ago, the Sassen had to be the ones to leave.*

Yar emerged from the bushes and inspected the tree break. He thought he knew what it meant, but he wanted to be absolutely sure. The one who had made the break was the first male Akassa he had ever seen. Akar'Tor did not count, having been raised at Kayerm. Earlier that day, Yar had also seen a female walking through. She looked similar to the Leader's mate, Hakani, though a little taller and more slender. He found their lack of hair covering disturbing; they looked as if they were walking about skinned alive. Yar wanted to get a closer look at them —meet them face to face—but the Sarnonn were forbidden to make contact with the Akassa, which made Yar nervous about being around them, so he kept himself hidden.

Yar went back and told Haan that the Locust trees were broken. The Akassa had asked for contact.

So soon? thought Haan. *I wonder what has happened*?

"Yar, go back and find the entrance to Kthama. You followed us when we first asked for their help. Ask for the Akassa named Khon'Tor, or the one called Acaraho. They will not harm you. Bring the message back to me, saying what they want."

"But Adik'Tar Haan, contact is forbidden. You have always told us that. And your father before you."

"I know. But they already know about us. So the contract has already been broken. We can only move forward, Yar, we cannot go back."

Yar stared, then nodded and reluctantly left for Kthama.

Acaraho was summoned to the Great Entrance. One of the Sarnonn had shown up.

"What did he say? What does he want?" Acaraho asked as they walked.

"I do not know," replied Awan. "He only said two

words, your name and Khon'Tor's. Since Khon'Tor is still sick, I came for you."

"Very well."

The Sarnonn was simply standing there in the entrance, hands to his side, unmoving. He held his head straight, only his eyes scanning the room.

Acaraho walked up to the giant. *I assume he is here because of the tree break.* He signed and spoke, "I am Acaraho, of the Akassa."

The Sarnonn looked down at Acaraho with his dark eyes. Acaraho steeled himself not to look away. *I have to control this reaction.*

"Haan sent me. You made the signal. What do you want?"

Acaraho signed back, "We need to speak with Haan. We need his help. I can go back with you to see him, or he can come here to see me.

Yar nodded, then walked away.

What the krell, thought Acaraho. *Well, I guess now we can only wait. And why did he look so nervous? They cannot be afraid of us. They must know they are far stronger than we are.*

Acaraho turned to First Guard Awan and the other males who were standing a few feet behind him.

"Awan. What did you see just now?" he asked, motioning after the Sarnonn.

"I saw a giant hair-covered beast of a male who had no business looking as afraid of you as he did. No offense, Commander—"

Acaraho chuckled, then added, "I saw it too. I cannot imagine. Is it possible they do not know how much stronger they are?"

The First Guard shook his head. "I have no idea, but he looked almost terrified. He stood there so stiff."

More mystery, thought Acaraho, and went to tell Khon'Tor they had made contact as hoped.

Yar returned to Haan and delivered the message.

"They cannot come here," Haan said. "I will go to them."

He had to tell Hakani he would be leaving for Kthama in a day or so to talk to Khon'Tor.

Akar'Tor jumped up from his place next to Haan, "I am going with you, Father!"

"Akar, you need to stay here with your mother and your sister."

"They have Haaka and Sastak to help them. That is female work. I want to come with you. How will I learn how to be a Leader if you keep me here with the *females*?"

Haan rubbed the back of his neck before answering. "I understand your desire to go there, but you cannot live in both worlds, Akar. You are going to have to forget about the People. But if it would help get them out of your system to go with me once more, then alright. But this will be the last time. Be ready when I am and go tell your mother."

"No!" said Hakani when Akar'Tor told her. "I do not want you to go back."

"I am sorry you do not like it, Mother, but I am going anyway." He hated to defy his mother, but he had made up his mind.

Haan listened and thought how stubborn his son was—just like Hakani. *I wonder if I have failed him in his upbringing. Both Hakani and Akar are difficult. Or maybe this is normal for the Akassa. None of us will ever be going back to Kthama again. I would never have made contact had it not been for Akar and Hakani's problems. When this is over, I will ignore any further requests for contact. I will explain it to one of their Leaders; I owe them that for the help they gave Akar and Hakani, but perhaps if I do not contact them again, the contract will stand.*

Then Haan remembered the Sassen's problems with their own future. No good choices. *It is a question of choosing the best of the worst. I admit that without their help, I have no solution to our problem.*

He sighed deeply.

Haan and Akar'Tor arrived at Kthama and were met by Acaraho and Awan.

"Thank you for coming. Khon'Tor is still not well, or he would have come to meet you himself," explained Acaraho while eyeing Akar'Tor. *Why is he here?*

Haan saw Acaraho looking Akar'Tor up and down.

"He asked to come along. He has a natural curiosity about the People and Kthama. However, this will be the last time he comes here. After this, contact between our people must cease."

I wonder what changed, Acaraho thought. "I am sorry to hear that, Haan. I feel we have much to learn from you."

Haan nodded, remembering it was their fault that Acaraho's community had gotten sick. As they were talking, Adia and Tehya arrived, looking for Acaraho. They stopped when they saw the two Sarnonn. Recognizing Akar'Tor by his silver crown, both females quickly swept the room to see if Hakani was with him. Not seeing her, Adia started toward Acaraho and Akar'Tor. Tehya put out a hand to stop her.

"Wait. Khon'Tor told me to stay away from them. I am leaving. He would be upset if he knew I did not obey him just because he is not around. I could not bear to lose his trust."

Adia nodded and watched Tehya go.

Akar'Tor had watched Tehya walking toward them and then turn around to leave. He felt himself reacting to her in a peculiar way. He slid his gaze over her figure, noticing she always wore wrappings and often some type of decoration around her neck. *Akassa females are different. They are not one shape all the way down. They have a bend in the middle, and they look different from the back and the front. She is younger than Khon'Tor; I think she is more my age than his.*

Once Tehya was gone, he turned his attention back to Haan and Acaraho.

"How long can you stay, Haan? We have many questions."

Haan looked at Akar'Tor, having seen his interest in Tehya. *Now I understand why he is so torn. Of course. He is past the age when he should have taken a mate. He has shown little interest in the females at Kayerm, not that any of them would have him. I should not be so quick to dismiss his interest. Perhaps his future lies with the Akassa.*

"We will stay long enough to speak with you and Khon'Tor," he answered.

Akar'Tor frowned but said nothing.

Acaraho led them through Kthama.

Haan looked once more at the smooth rock walls, the ample walkways. Heads turned as they walked into the eating area. *Their life is different from ours. They spend more time together in group activities, like eating together. There is much we could learn from their ways. Now I am again unsure about which path to take with them.*

"Would you like to eat? I can have someone look for Khon'Tor while you do."

Haan nodded. "Thank you."

Acaraho arranged to have one of the females bring them a selection of food and sat down with the visitors to keep them company as they ate. Adia left to tell Khon'Tor that the Sarnonn Leader was there.

"I apologize that my people keep staring at you. They do not mean any disrespect. I imagine that Hakani was also probably a curiosity within your community at first," offered Acaraho.

"Yes. I do not take offense. We are quite different in some ways. Not so much in others."

"Thank you for coming back. I regret there was conflict when you were here before. Hakani and Khon'Tor have a difficult history together. Perhaps without her here—"

"I understand, Commander. No more words are necessary. Now, why did you ask me to come back so soon?"

"We do have questions, but if you do not mind, I would prefer that the others are present as well. If you would like to enjoy your food, I will gather those who need to hear what you have to say."

Haan nodded and went back to eating.

Before long, Acaraho returned to collect him and Akar'Tor.

"Khon'Tor is ready for you now. Please come with

me. We will meet in his quarters; he is still recovering, but wants to speak with you."

○

Khon'Tor forced himself to get up out of bed and sit up to meet with Haan. It was all he could do to maintain a sitting position. He was not happy that Akar'Tor had also come, and he did not like having them there, in his own quarters. But he had overextended himself earlier and now felt too weak to go anywhere else. He also did not want to start anew on the wrong footing by asking Akar'Tor to leave.

So many things have changed. People coming and going in the Healer's Quarters—and now here? It cannot continue.

"I am going to visit Mapiya," Tehya said. "I do not think you want me here while they are present."

"Stay, Tehya." Khon'Tor reached up and grabbed her wrist. "I was mostly worried about you being in the same room as Hakani. You are Third Rank. You need to hear what I am going to ask Haan."

Tehya sat back down next to her mate and squeezed his hand.

Khon'Tor wanted her with him. He did not want her wandering about with the Sarnonn here. At least while they were all in the room with him, he could keep track of them. *There are no good choices right now. But at least Hakani had the good sense not to return with them. I made it clear she was not welcome here, ever again.*

Acaraho led Haan and Akar'Tor through the rock tunnels, making several turns before coming to the Leader's Quarters, then ushered them in.

"Thank you for coming. Please sit; join us." Khon'Tor added Handspeak to his words, as Adia had done before.

Akar'Tor smiled at seeing Tehya there. He looked around the quarters, taking in the expansive arrangements. *So, this is where he lives with her. And where are the other females in his pod?*

I wonder if all the living pods are this big; Kthama is so much bigger than Kayerm. Why do they have dried flowers in here? And why the fluorite and amethyst? They seem to serve no purpose. Akar'Tor studied the room, taking note of the doorways, the tables, the sleeping area. Again, he could not help staring at Tehya.

Kweeuu stayed at Tehya's side, and without raising his head, he growled at Akar'Tor. Tehya reached down and wrapped her hand around his muzzle, telling him to hush.

"I was not able to go with you before," Khon'Tor said, "but Acaraho told me of your conversation in the valley. I wanted to speak with you more about that. You spoke of the Mothoc and the Wrak-Wavara."

"Yes, the Mothoc, the Fathers-Of-Us-All," Haan answered.

"Are there any of the Mothoc still around?"

"Of this, I cannot speak, Khon'Tor."

Is he saying he is not allowed to speak of it, or is Haan saying he does not know? "Then, perhaps we may speak of the Wrak-Wavara. It is common knowledge among the Sassen?"

"The history between our people, yes, though we are not supposed to make contact with you. If it had not been for Akar'Tor and Hakani, we would most likely have never come together. I struggled with that decision, but what is done is done."

Khon'Tor and Acaraho quickly glanced at each other.

"No contact between us? Did you know we were here before Hakani stopped our scout?"

"Yes, all the Sassen know about the Akassa. The Sassen and the Akassa used to live here together, at Kthama. My people left Kthama and went to live at Kayerm. Kayerm is our home now. Hakani's home, and Akar'Tor's home. We knew of Kthama, but the location was concealed from us. Only when Hakani led us here, did we learn where it was."

Silence descended as Khon'Tor and Acaraho took in what he had just said.

Haan turned to Akar'Tor and saw that he was staring hungrily at Tehya. "Akar'Tor, I need you to leave the room now, while I speak with the Akassa Leaders."

Akar'Tor scowled but rose and did as he was told.

Khon'Tor watched as his near-double left. Once the young male was gone, Haan turned back to the group.

"Akar insisted on coming back with me. I feared that bringing him here before would confuse him, but he and Hakani both needed your help. He should have been paired by now, but he is not interested in our females. Maybe you can understand his interest in coming. He seeks his place in the world."

"We all understand that," Adia said. "Oh'Dar, the Waschini offspring I rescued, has the same struggle. He was raised as one of us, the Akassa, but he is not one of us. Now that he is grown, he does not know where he belongs, either. So yes, we do understand."

Haan nodded. "Khon'Tor, our laws forbid contact between our two tribes. However, now that contact has been made, the damage is already done. I cannot undo the past. I do not foresee any problems between us, though. Do you have concerns?"

Khon'Tor inhaled and let his breath out slowly. *He is being candid; he has been nothing but forthcoming. Hakani is the one who was deceitful, and our problems only arose when she became involved, and I lost my temper. They are far more powerful; if they wanted to harm us, they would have done so already. We need to establish good relationships with them, and here is our chance.*

"We have no prohibition about contact with you," Khon'Tor said. "I agree; I, too, see no trouble between us. We, as a people, are facing some challenges about which you may have information that could help us solve them. We have a High Council meeting coming up soon. The High Council is made up of Leaders from all the different tribes and communities. I would like you to stay—or return—and meet with them."

"Yes, the Council, the many Leaders from different tribes. Are they still all Akassa?"

Haan speaks as if he knows of the High Council, Khon'Tor noted.

"Many of them are. Some are of the Brothers. They look like the Waschini, only darker. They live not far from the edge of our territory."

"The Others," said Haan.

*The Brothers—the Others—*close, thought Khon'Tor. "Leader to Leader, Haan, I need your help. You have information about the history of our peoples that the Akassa do not have. Whatever you can tell us will help with the serious challenges that we are facing as a people. Without hearing what you know, we have no idea what else we may have wrong. And the High Council must hear first hand whatever you can share with us. Remember that we believed the Sarnonn no longer walked Etera, and we know nothing of the Mothoc. We need you to tell the High

Council everything you know about the Wrak-Wavara and our shared history."

"The Others were left to the Akassa."

Khon'Tor frowned, not understanding what was behind Haan's statement and the concern in his voice. *Why does he keep coming back to this? Do they perhaps also have laws forbidding contact with the Brothers? Is that the problem?*

"The Others will not be at this High Council meeting."

Haan nodded.

That seemed to satisfy him, thought Khon'Tor.

"How long before your High Council meets?"

"During the heat of summer—not long."

Haan looked off into space. Khon'Tor gave him time. *I can see he is struggling with this decision.*

After what seemed like an insufferably long period of silence, Haan finally answered, "I will come back at that time. You do not need to make another tree break. Just peel the bark lower on the two Locust trees you already marked."

"That brings up a question; have you always had watchers in the valley?" asked Acaraho.

"Watchers? What we call sentries? No. We have avoided what we believed to be your territory to avoid any chance of exposing our people to yours. I only placed a sentry here after we made contact with your watcher," Haan explained.

"Do the Others know that you exist?" Acaraho

asked Khon'Tor's question, having earlier seen the frown on the Leader's face.

"Perhaps in the far reaches of Etera. Here, we do not make contact with them. But they knew the Mothoc existed, though there was seldom contact. The Mothoc were the keepers of the Others. They protected them, shielded them, provided for them in ways of which the Others were never aware. But we —we have kept to ourselves since the end of the age."

Acaraho nodded.

"We will go back. When it is time for me to return, I will be ready. If you do not mind, I may bring Akar back with me. I will tell you and the High Council members more when I return."

"Haan, before you go, do you have a Healer there at your home? I want to send back some medicine for Hakani. It will help her feel better," said Adia.

"We do. But I am sure he will appreciate your help."

"I will be right back."

"Thank you, everyone," said Khon'Tor.

Acaraho stood up as a signal for Haan, and they stepped out of the Leader's Quarters. Akar'Tor was sitting in the hallway against the stone wall, waiting for them.

He jumped up when he saw his father and Acaraho exit the Leader's Quarters.

"Are we leaving already?" he asked, trotting after them.

"Yes. I do not like leaving your mother alone with the young one. I will be back another time."

"Will I get to come with you?"

"We will see," Haan replied.

Acaraho said, "If you wait here, I will fetch the medicine that Adia wished to send for Hakani."

When Acaraho was out of sight, Akar'Tor turned back to his father, "Please let me come back with you next time."

"Most likely, I will allow it, Akar. But a lot can happen between now and then, and you must try to understand if I change my mind. I do not know what will happen at this meeting they are calling. If you come, you will have to occupy yourself while I am busy with the other Leaders."

Haan sighed. *I keep vacillating between going back to Kayerm and forgetting we ever found Kthama, to moving forward and establishing close ties with these Akassa. I am not sure my people will survive without their help, yet by making contact, I am risking everything. If I do not decide, the time will come when it is too late to change my course, and the decision will have been made for me. I fear that too much time may already have passed. I may be committed to this path, whether I agree with it now or not.*

"I do not mind, Father. I can find someone to talk with, perhaps others my age."

Akar'Tor's voice shook Haan out of his deep thought.

Acaraho and Adia returned together. Adia handed Haan a small pouch with herbs in it. "You can tell your Healer it is Nettle and Chamomile. He will most likely recognize it."

Acaraho walked down the hallway with the Sarnonn and Akar'Tor. He noticed the young male looking down the adjoining corridors on the way back out.

"Akar'Tor, I heard you talking when I approached. I would be glad to introduce you to others around your age if you do return."

"Thank you, Acaraho. I hope I get to come back."

Acaraho and Adia watched the visitors leave before returning to Khon'Tor's quarters.

❁

Khon'Tor was clearly exhausted, but he forced himself to sit up again when Acaraho and Adia returned.

"That was interesting, was it not?" said Acaraho. "It concerns me that they have more of the story of the Wrak-Wavara than we do. Or at least, more of the story than has been shared with us. Whether that is intentional or whether our people never had the knowledge, I have no way of knowing.

"I do not know how this helps us with our future

problems. But it is information we did not have. Perhaps something will come of it. The High Council asked each community to try to locate any Sarnonn tribes. We will find out at the High Council if any of the others have been as lucky as we. Based on Haan's remarks about not wanting his people to cross our paths, we most likely would not have done so, had it not been for Hakani and Akar'Tor needing our help," he continued.

"Adia, thank you for sending the herbs to Hakani. That was a goodwill gesture," said Khon'Tor.

"It is my responsibility to help where I can. I do not get to choose, depending on whether I like the person or not," Adia said. "It is possible she will just throw out the herbs I sent. But that is out of my control."

Acaraho smiled at his mate and rubbed her back.

"Tehya, while we were talking to him, what did you see?" asked Khon'Tor.

She exhaled and took a moment before replying. "Akar'Tor kept looking around the room the whole time you were talking. He was interested in everything. I believe that many of the items in here are unfamiliar to him, such as the dried flowers, baskets, our decorative rocks. He was also very interested in you, Khon'Tor. And in me. Whenever I caught him looking at me, he would go back to looking at you. I am sure it is just natural curiosity."

"Maybe so. I also noticed it. I do not like it. Acaraho, when—if—Akar'Tor comes back, make sure that Tehya is well guarded again. He may be harmless—he did protect us against Haan. But remember who raised him. And I regret that he knows where our quarters are."

Acaraho nodded and looked at Tehya, who had glanced away. "Tehya, Khon'Tor is right. As angry as Hakani is at us still, some of that had to contaminate his thinking. He may well be torn about whether or not he belongs with our people, but we cannot know for sure what has been going through his mind all this time. What else did you notice?"

"While Akar'Tor was interested in the room, Haan was not. He scanned it once, quickly. It may just be that as a Leader, he was focused on you—or he may have been relaxed and had no concerns about his surroundings."

"Again, being the most powerful in any setting tends to allow one to relax," Acaraho remarked.

"Adia, any observations from your seventh sense?"

"Haan is as he appears. He was candid and genuine. The trouble between you over Hakani is gone. He wants to ally himself with you, but as he said, he has considerable struggle over their prohibition against contact. I wish we had more time with him. There are so many questions."

"Yes. I did not want to keep firing them at him. It is confusing and troublesome that there is so much we do not know about the past. I expected him to stay longer," Acaraho said.

"I felt Haan did want to get back to Hakani; he is

concerned about her. I am sure she is still stirred up from her stay here," said Adia. "But there is more. Haan wants something from us too, but he is struggling with whether to ask for our help or not."

"Do you know what it might be?" asked Acaraho.

"Only that it has to do with the Wrak-Wavara. I believe there is a good chance he will bring it up at the High Council meeting."

"So, our history is wrong," Khon'Tor said. "We are not the result of the Sarnonn mating with the Brothers. The Mothoc bred with the Others, who I am positive were probably the earlier Brothers. And I said we had no prohibition on contact with the Sarnonn, but what if they were originally included in our Second Law: No Contact With Outsiders?" asked Khon'Tor.

"But we have called them the Sarnonn for generations. Whether they would have been mentioned specifically or merely included in the term Outsiders, I do not know," said Acaraho, shaking his head.

Adia put in, "But the High Council members specifically asked us all to look for them. The High Council Leaders are among the few with any knowledge of the Wrak-Wavara. They would not knowingly tell us to look for them if contact was also forbidden from our side. *Would they*?"

Khon'Tor sighed. "These are all good questions for which we have no answers at present."

Adia rose and stepped over to him, "May I?" she

asked before laying the back of her hand against his forehead. "We need to leave and let you get rested. I will be glad to bring you both something to eat."

"I will go; let me walk with you. Khon'Tor, I will be back in a little bit," said Tehya, jumping to join Adia and Acaraho.

In the hallway, Tehya asked Adia, "Is he getting worse or better?"

"He is getting better. But he resists his rest, and that is dragging out his recovery. He seems more relaxed when you are with him."

"Yes, he worries when we are apart. I am not sure why."

"I can tell you why, Tehya," said Adia with a smile. "It is because he truly loves you. You are everything to him. Before you, it was his position that mattered. Being Leader of the People was the most important thing to Khon'Tor. It was his passion. Now —it is you."

CHAPTER 3

The sunset at Kthama was just as beautiful as it would be thousands of years later in Khon'Tor's time. The Mothoc counted themselves deeply blessed by the Great Spirit to live in such an expansive underground system situated amid a land rich and overflowing with blessings. Moc'Tor breathed in the humid air drifting up from the Great River below, his heavy, full-body silver coat tinged a pale orange by the setting rays. His coloring was unusual among his people, the mark of a Guardian. *Cooler days are coming; it will be a relief to us all.*

Moc'Tor turned from the view as his First Choice approached. "It is time," he sighed. "There are difficult times ahead, E'ranale. I can feel it. The Order of Functions is requiring more and more of my strength than ever before. Pray that I have the wisdom to guide our people successfully through the storm that is coming."

E'ranale looked at her mate. As the Leader of High Rocks, his responsibilities were tremendous. Add in the fact that he was also the Guardian, and she could only imagine the pressure he felt. Like all the Mothoc, the flow of the Aezaitera coursed through her own veins. The Aezaitera was the very creative life force of the Great Spirit—the breath of life continuously entering and exiting Etera's realm.

But E'ranale was not a Guardian. Her physical body was not a vehicle called to bear the burden of supporting the Order of Functions, the creative blueprint of the Great Mind, which was constantly adjusting and reordering to maintain the perfect orchestration of life in their realm.

She placed her hand on his shoulder. "I can see that something has been taking its toll on you. Come. Let us get this over with. We can rest together at the end of the day, and I will minister to you."

The Great Chamber of Kthama was filled to capacity. Moc'Tor started to push a way through to the front to address his people, a path opening as they realized he was coming forward. As he stood at the front, hundreds of pairs of deep-set eyes stared back at him, waiting for him to speak. The huge room was a sea of dark-haired bodies, crushed together shoulder-to-shoulder. He could barely tell where one began and the other ended. When one moved, the others pressed against them had to move in unison. Ordinarily, it would not have been this crowded, but both the males and the females were assembled together for this announcement.

With the thick bark-covered Leader's Staff grasped firmly, Moc'Tor stepped up onto the raised platform he always used when addressing the crowd. "I am not sure everyone is here, but no matter. If anyone is absent, you can tell them later about today's announcement. If you look around, you will see that our community has grown considerably since my father handed the rule over to me. Unfortunately, it will not be long before we reach Kthama's limits. It is time we face the fact that we must look for another home. Scouts are out now as I speak. My hope is that they will find a place not too far from here where we can all share Kthama's bounty. Our food stores are full, but we have a long winter ahead, and we are in a race against time to expand our living space."

Moc'Tor stepped closer to the crowd but remained on the raised platform. "Does anyone have any questions?"

Toniss spoke up from the front row, "Are we leaving Kthama, Adik'Tar?"

"I doubt we will find another place that is big enough for us to leave Kthama together. We are hoping to find another dwelling nearby so that we can keep our community together even though some of us will relocate."

"How will it be decided who leaves here?" continued Toniss. "We have relationships, family."

"I do not yet know. But I will do my best to be fair."

The Mothoc looked at each other. Moc'Tor could see the furrowed brows over their dark eyes.

"But we have always lived here; this is our home, Guardian," Toniss said.

"I know it is not easy to accept," Moc'Tor addressed the young female. "It will be hard for those who must leave. But we will still be one people."

Dochrohan, First Guard, approached to stand with Moc'Tor. His heavy dark hair covering contrasted sharply with Moc'Tor's silver-white Guardian's coat.

"Our stories tell us that we have always lived here," Moc'Tor went on. "But we can no longer hold onto what was. We do know this area is rich with unexplored hillsides. We have never needed to look for another cave system, but I am confident we will find something suitable for expansion.

"I will not order you to stop mating, but until we find more space, I am hard-put to justify the wisdom in continuing to reproduce. We do not know how long it will take to find another livable space. When we do, it will no doubt have to be modified. In the meantime, every offling decreases the living space for us all. I will let you know as soon as I have something to report."

Moc'Tor finished his speech with a few words of encouragement and stepped down. The crowd parted just enough for him to pass through. Even as one of the tallest of the Mothoc, Moc'Tor felt smothered as he pressed his way through all the bodies.

After much discussion, the crowd dispersed, glad to be freed from the cramped assembly.

E'ranale, First Guard Dochrohan, and Oragur, the Healer, weaved through the crowd, following the Leader outside, where they stood to speak.

"Quite a bit of talk afterward," Moc'Tor said. "It is obvious no one wants to leave Kthama. Who can blame them? We are blessed with our extensive tunnel system, the Mother Stream that sweeps through our lower level bringing fresh water and air, the large number of smaller caves for separate living spaces."

"This is their home," E'ranale said. "This is all they have known. As far back as memory goes, their parents and their parents' parents walked and lived within these same walls."

Moc'Tor paused, lost in thought, before continuing. "When did the last scouts go out?"

It was Dochrohan who spoke. "Two days ago. It is a long process. But I am confident we will find something. Like Kthama, any other entrances might be covered over and difficult to find."

"That is a good point, Dochrohan," said Moc'Tor.

"But I doubt there will be another location with as rich a vortex as that beneath us here. Now, I have decided to visit the other colonies up the Mother Stream to see if they are also nearing capacity. I should be leaving in a few days."

"The crowd has probably dispersed; do you want to go back inside?" he asked E'ranale as Dochrohan and Oragur left.

"Not yet. I prefer it out here; the fresh air is a gift." She paused. "Toniss is seeded again."

Moc'Tor sighed. "I cannot bring myself to order them not to mate."

"It would be a hard adjustment. The males have always mated whenever they want to. I am not sure what the females would say, but many of them are tired of being constantly seeded, I can tell you that much." E'ranale took a deep breath. "My mate, there is no good time to tell you this, but I am also seeded."

Moc'Tor knew he should be happy, but this was not good news. Especially after telling his people they were near capacity and that more offling only added to the problem. But he did not want to hurt his mate's feelings.

He forced a smile.

"I am sorry," she said.

"It is not your fault, E'ranale. Only the Great Spirit decides when the male's seed will take root and produce an offling. And if anyone is at fault, it is me for not being able to stay off you," he said.

E'ranale was his First Choice. His two other

mates lived with her in the smaller cave system next to Kthama. Only during assemblies like today's did the males and females mix freely. At least, now that E'ranale was seeded, he could mate with her at will. Later on, when the time came that E'ranale was too uncomfortable, he could pick one of his other females to mate if need be. But I need to abstain from the others, considering our problem. Moc'Tor knew it would not be difficult for him; it was only E'ranale whom he truly desired.

Dochrohan, First Guard, approached to stand with Moc'Tor. His heavy dark hair covering contrasted sharply with Moc'Tor's almost silver-white Guardian coat.

Moc'Tor stood nearly fourteen feet tall, with broad shoulders atop a thick muscular core. There was little that could stand in his way. His heavy coat provided protection from the coldest winter elements. All the Mothoc suffered in the warm weather.

He ran his hand over the back of his head and smoothed the top of his hair, a habit he had picked up from his father. There was no mistaking Moc'Tor, with his silver coloring. None of his offspring, as of yet, had been born Guardians, no matter which female he mated.

His special status made him particularly attractive to the females, who frequently offered themselves to him. However, for some time now, Moc'Tor had limited his mating to three. E'ranale was his First

Choice, and as time passed, he had stopped mating with his Second and Third Choice unless they presented themselves to him. He was content with E'ranale, and they shared far more than a relationship of physical release. She was more than his mate; she was his friend, his confidant, and in many ways, his chief counsel. He would choose his successor from her offling, although, in the lifespan of a Guardian, Moc'Tor was still very young.

While they were still talking, Drit came out to set the wood for the evening fire. The Mothoc did not allow fire within the cave system of Kthama. Smoke accumulated at the top of the caves was difficult to clear since there was little circulation other than whatever breeze came up from the Mother Stream. But one of Moc'Tor's favorite ways to relax was sitting around a fire at night, enjoying the canopy of stars that blanketed the dark sky, even in warmer weather. It was perfectly safe, for the Mothoc had few natural predators, and hardly any had ever known fear.

Before long, Drit had a roaring fire going, sparked to life using his flint and striking stones. He always carried them in a pouch slung over his shoulder. Drit was the Fixer, the chief toolmaker, and brother to Oragur the Healer.

The last star to appear found them and a few others still sitting around the fire talking. "What if we cannot find another dwelling, Moc'Tor?" asked Oragur.

"If we cannot, then we will have to limit mating.

It will be an unpopular directive and one I am not sure they will follow. The males are used to mating whenever they wish. Perhaps by the time I get back from visiting the other communities, our scouts will have returned with good news. Even if we split the community into different living areas, we still need to address the uncontrolled seeding of the females, or in a few generations from now, we will be right back where we are."

"If they report they have found a place before you return, what is your wish?"

"Move forward. Take a party and examine the place more closely. See what modifications would have to be made and report to me when I return. There is no use wasting time while I am away," replied Moc'Tor.

E'ranale rose to leave. "I am returning to my quarters."

"Stay with me tonight," said Moc'Tor. "There is now no harm in doing so."

E'ranale nodded. "As you wish. Wake me when you come in; I am going to rest."

"Why do you not mate with Ushca or Ny'on?" asked Oragur once E'ranale had left.

"This is the problem, Oragur. If I turn to Ushca and Ny'on, they will get seeded again. We are in this situation because we have no mastery over our desires. Our females are constantly having offling. Perhaps after I return from the other communities, I will have some new ideas about how to deal with it.

At least some of them must be facing the same challenge."

The Mothoc stayed within their own communities for the most part. There was no conflict between them as the land was rich with resources and no need for competition. As a race, they were peaceful. Though the Mothoc were bound to protect and care for their neighbors, the Others, the two groups had virtually no contact. The Mothoc's seldom let themselves be known to the Others, and they shared no common language. The Others knew nothing of the extent to which the Mothoc watched over them, on both natural and spiritual levels.

A visit to the other Mothoc communities, especially by the Guardian, would stir much talk and concern. As a result, Moc'Tor rarely undertook it.

He tossed some acorns into the flames, watching the embers scatter as they landed. "I will see you at daybreak, then," he said to Oragur. He rose and retired to his quarters where E'ranale was already sleeping.

She woke when he slipped in next to her on the thick mass of grass and leaves.

"Do you wish to mate, Moc'Tor?" she asked, rubbing her eyes and rolling over toward him.

"No, not tonight. I want to talk to you. Get your ideas as the speaker for the females."

E'ranale propped herself up on one elbow.

"There are too many of us. And I do not know how to stop it," Moc'Tor said. "There is no guarantee we will find another cave system to meet our needs. At the rate we are going, we will be impossibly overcrowded in one more generation. Is there any talk among the females about this?"

"The females know it is getting crowded. They worry, too, about what will happen. But the males do not let up on them. The moment one of them becomes seeded, they mate with another. It feels like all we do is produce offling, one after the other."

"I am open to ideas," he answered, pulling her in close to him.

"I am afraid the males will not support any change. But I believe the females would."

"What if, for the time being, a male can only ever mate with one specific female?"

E'ranale remained silent, considering the thought. "That would certainly cut down on the seedings."

"Yes, although it would not be a very popular decision. But if it were only for a short time until we find another living space—"

"You know the males better than I do, but I think it will take a compelling argument or a strong hand to convince some of them. The females will support it, but it seems we have no say."

"What do you mean?"

"Well, if a male wants to mate, we have no choice but to comply. That is the way it has always been."

Moc'Tor sat in silence for a moment. I never

looked at it from their viewpoint. It did not occur to me they might want to refuse.

"The females do not want to mate?"

"It is not that we do not want to mate, but we get tired of being seeded all the time. And we do not necessarily want to mate with just any male. We have preferences, too, just as you do. I am grateful to be able to accept only you."

Moc'Tor released his arm from around her, stood up, and paced back and forth. "What if it were the female who got to choose?"

"Got to choose what? To mate?"

"Not only whether to mate, but with whom to mate. What if it were the female's choice who to mate with—or not?"

E'ranale blinked a few times. "Oh, Moc'Tor, that would be such a relief. But I doubt you can sell that idea to the males. And what if more than one male favored the same female?"

"It would be the female's choice; that would be the end of it because we cannot continue as we are. I will think about this some more." He lay down again.

"Are you sure you do not wish to mate?" she smiled.

Moc'Tor let his eyes wander over his First Choice; her warm scent was inviting. He felt his response to her offer. "E'ranale. If it were up to you, would you choose me?"

"I would always choose you, Moc'Tor. And only you." She smiled again and pulled him closer.

Afterward, E'ranale kept thinking about Moc'Tor's idea and could not get to sleep. Having a say in who they mated with would be a great relief to the females. Some of them had feelings for particular males, and it was the same way for many of the males. If those who wished to limit their mating to only one other were given the choice, many hard feelings would be alleviated. But she would say nothing to the females yet for fear of getting their hopes up.

Because the females and offling lived in a smaller cave system adjacent to the males' larger one, their total numbers were deceiving. However, the assembly that day with all the males, females, and offling had shown just how overgrown their population was. In her head, E'ranale went through the females one by one, trying to figure out just how many would prefer to be paired to one specific male. She decided it was about three-quarters of the population. However, she could see conflict erupting when more than one male favored the same female, even though it would be the female's choice.

Morning came and found Moc'Tor thinking over his idea. Change came hard to the Mothoc, but if they were to survive, change they must.

E'ranale rolled over and found him sitting next to her. "Good morning. Have you been awake long?"

"Yes. I have been thinking about what we discussed. As I announced, I am going to travel along the Mother Stream to the Deep Valley and the Far High Hills and talk to their Leaders. I will take the Healer with me."

Moc'Tor and Oragur followed the Mother Stream to the next population, a small establishment named Khire, of only a handful of Mothoc. Past that was the Deep Valley, a day or so's travel further along the Mother Stream. Although visits to other communities were rare, many years past, the Mothoc had worked on the passageway along the route, carving out places to stop and rest, even to sleep. They had also created markings on the walls along the path to indicate to the traveler how far it was to the next community. Along the route, there were exit points to the surface, though they were few and far between. With a constant supply of fresh water, it was not difficult to travel, though being cut off from the topside for considerable stretches sometimes made it hard to tell day from night.

Moc'Tor and Oragur surfaced and checked the area for the tree breaks, the markers used by their people to signal the way to the small community named Khire. They quickly located them and traveled in the direction indicated. Before too long, they sensed the presence of the other Mothoc.

"I am Moc'Tor, Leader of the People of the High Rocks," he called out. "And this is Oragur the Healer, also from the High Rocks. We would like to speak with whoever you acknowledge as Adik'Tar."

As if by magic, three shapes stepped from the shadows. At seeing Moc'Tor, they exchanged glances before greeting him and Oragur.

"We will take you to him, Guardian," said the tallest, his face revealing his concern that a Guardian would be paying them a visit.

After traveling through the brush and up a slight incline, they came to a concealed opening—a small entrance compared to that of Kthama. A fire was being tended just inside, adding a warm glow to the otherwise gloomy interior. Before long, a shorter, stocky male approached, hobbling somewhat.

"I am Cha'Kahn. I am the highest rank here. Welcome to Khire. Visitors are an infrequent occurrence, and a visit by a Guardian even less frequent. What is your business?"

"I am Moc'Tor, and this is Oragur. We live downstream at the High Rocks. I am traveling to other tribes to seek counsel."

"Come, sit by the fire," said Cha'Kahn.

The two joined him around the dancing flames, which were welcome after the time spent in the dank tunnels along the Mother Stream. In the back reaches of the cave, both Moc'Tor and Oragur could see a number of females tending to figures stretched out on sleeping mats. Another female approached with a gourd and gave each one something to drink, one after another.

"Are you hungry?" asked Cha'Kahn.

"Thank you, but we are fine. Our problem is difficult to solve, Adik'Tar. We are outgrowing our mother caves. Are you facing the same problem?"

"We were, but we solved the problem by putting limits on mating."

"That has been my thought. But how did you get them to agree?"

As Cha'Kahn spoke, Moc'Tor's gaze kept shifting to the activity at the back of the cave. "It was difficult at first. Those who were unhappy left to find other communities. Since then, we have not had this problem, but I made the decree before it got out of hand."

"I am afraid we are past that point already," Moc'Tor sighed.

"I have heard of your community. Yours is the largest known."

Moc'Tor sat for a moment. While he was thinking, another figure was brought in and laid on the mats. Some females bent over solicitously, apparently trying to soothe the obvious discomfort.

"Would you be willing to meet with the other Adik'Tars?" asked Moc'Tor. "We could help each other with such problems if we band together."

"I would not object to that. The mantle of leadership borne alone is sometimes heavy."

Not able to ignore it any longer, and since Cha'Kahn was not going to volunteer the information, Moc'Tor had to ask. "You seem to have quite a few who are ill."

"Yes, but it is just a low fever and a bit of pain. We do not know what is causing it."

Moc'Tor tried to quell his unease over the number who were sick, but he felt a need to leave as soon as possible. After a bit more talk, he thanked Cha'Kahn, and he and Oragur continued on their way to the Deep Valley.

"Did you notice the number being cared for back there?" asked Moc'Tor as they walked.

"I found it a little disturbing, yes. They likely ate something the essence of which had long before returned to the Great Spirit, but I did not want to pry."

❁

As Moc'Tor and Oragur arrived at the Deep Valley, the Guardian noted that the surroundings were even lusher than those at Kthama. His father had once told him this was the second-largest underground cave system, next only to that of the High Rocks. Those who lived there enjoyed a life of relative ease and plenty. As they approached, watchers greeted him and Oragur just as those at Cha'Kahn's settlement had done. Before long, they were engaged in a similar conversation with Hatos'Mok.

"I have no answers for you, Guardian," said the Leader of the community of the Deep Valley. "I believe you will find that all our people struggle with the risk of overpopulation. We have practically no natural enemies. Other than an occasional accident, most of us live out our natural lifespans until it is time to return to the Great Spirit."

Moc'Tor sighed. "I suspect I will find the same response at the Far High Hills."

"I know the Leader there; his name is Tres'Sar. Yes, you will find similar overcrowded conditions."

Moc'Tor noticed a parade of young females walking slowly through the area close to where he, Oragur, and Hatos'Mok were talking.

"It appears you can have your choice of females, Guardian," Hatos'Mok remarked, his eyes on the attractive maidens who were not even trying to hide their fascination with the Guardian.

"I have three to mate; they are all I need for my satisfaction. And I do not wish to add to the surplus population. But from what I can see, I will say that your maidens are particularly attractive."

Hatos'Mok nodded. "There are also three in my pod, though I find I have my favorite."

"I am considering bringing the leadership together to see if we can find solutions," Moc'Tor said. "If you are open to that, I will send a messenger when we are ready to convene."

Hatos'Mok agreed and offered Moc'Tor and Oragur lodging for the night.

The next morning the travelers left for the Far High Hills and met with Tres'Sar, garnering his support for the idea of coming together to solve their problems.

The sentries had returned by the time Moc'Tor and Oragur made it back to Kthama.

"Moc'Tor," said the head sentry, Ras'Or, "We have located a set of caves not all that far away from here. It is not as large as Kthama, but it is well-concealed and looks serviceable. We almost missed it because the opening was so well-hidden by bittersweet vines. There is a stream not far away, and there is plenty of cover."

"Do you believe it will suit our needs?"

"It will not be as comfortable as Kthama, but we can improve it—although it will take some time."

"How many do you think could live there comfortably?"

"Perhaps a fourth of our population."

"Are you sure there are no others?" asked Moc'Tor.

"None that we can find, and we have been diligent in our search."

Moc'Tor considered what Ras'Or had just said. Not entirely big enough, but it will buy us some time. Now he would have to decide who must leave

Kthama. "Please take me there; I must inspect it myself."

That evening, after telling E'ranale he was leaving again and would not be back for several days, Moc'Tor gathered his hunting spear, collected Oragur and Drit, and set out with Ras'Or.

Darkness being no hindrance to them, they traveled with few rests and arrived just before first light on the next day. Ras'Or was right; the new cave system was virtually undiscoverable.

Moc'Tor set aside his hunting spear and pushed aside the covering that blocked most of the entrance. Later they could decide what to leave in place and what to cultivate further. Though they had few natural enemies, concealment provided some level of comfort.

The opening expanded into an entrance similar to that at Kthama, though on a smaller scale. From the main cave, tunnels extended in multiple directions. Moc'Tor chose the narrowest and set out along it with Drit and Oragur in tow.

The air was cool but not as humid as at Kthama. Moc'Tor knew from the dryness that there was no central stream running through the caves, though off in the distance on the way there, they had spotted the river mentioned by Ras'Or. The Mother Stream made life at Kthama convenient. Not only did it bring water, oxygen, and nutrients into their home, but it carried an easy supply of protein in the fish that swam through. It was a shame that the Mother Stream did not also run beneath this underground cave system.

Moc'Tor followed the narrow tunnel with its familiar smooth rock walls. At its end, the passageway opened into several other caves. He turned to Drit, "Go back and take the next tunnel over. Oragur, you take the farthest. Walk about the same distance as we have here, then meet me back in the central area with a report. Look for signs of water, other exits, current or former inhabitants—anything good or bad. I will see you again shortly."

The two males did as ordered. Before long, they were all reassembled in the front cavern.

"The next tunnel was essentially the same as the first," Drit reported. "It wound around with several smaller caves along the way. There would be room for many single or shared quarters. I do not see an easy way to separate the females from the males, though."

"We would not want to send only males or only females here," mused Moc'Tor. "It has to be a mix like at Kthama. Oragur, what did you find?"

"Though Drit's tunnel does not sound suitable for both males and females, the route I took forked into two tunnels a short way back. I did not have time to explore both, but there may be a way to separate them by using that split."

Moc'Tor nodded. "Very well. Any signs of inhabitants?"

Both males shook their heads. It was no problem for the Mothoc to remove any creature already living there, but they would not wish to deprive any of the Great Spirit's creatures of a home.

"I want to see the river," Moc'Tor said, and with that, they left the caves and headed toward the water.

It was clearly part of the Great River that also wove past Kthama. Moc'Tor felt a sense of continuity, the two locations connected by the same rich source of life and provision. In addition, this place was not as high up as Kthama, so there were none of the rocky outcrops that made travel around Kthama treacherous. Mature trees provided a canopy of shade, and the breeze from the river brought with it the smell of the rich soil along the riverbanks.

The three males stood for a while, connecting with their seventh sense to feel if the place welcomed them. Though this was not as strong in them as it was in the females, they could still feel the whisper of the Great Spirit speaking to them. Each searched for a sense of foreboding or a warning of any sort.

Moments passed.

Moc'Tor exhaled. He opened his eyes at the same time the others did. The three nodded to each other, intuitively knowing it was settled. This would be their next home; the Great Spirit had once again provided.

"There is no rich magnetic vortex here as there is

below Kthama," conceded Moc'Tor. "But it will do. Let us stay the night; we can easily spear some fish and make a small fire. It will be our ritual of gratitude for this gift from the One-Who-Is-Three."

Before long, Drit had a warm fire going. With their bellies full, the males looked up at the wash of stars overhead. In the morning, they started out on their return to Kthama.

CHAPTER 4

E'ranale was anxiously awaiting her mate's return. She smiled at the sight of Moc'Tor coming up the rocky path to home.

"I was just going out to gather some berries."

"I will walk with you," said Moc'Tor, handing his spear to Drit and signaling for the other males to go on without him.

He went ahead, brushing the branches out of the way for E'ranale, a courtesy more than anything as she was certainly capable of making her own path.

"What did you think of it, Moc'Tor?" she asked.

"It is a blessing to find something so relatively close. It is large enough and has quite a few branches for separate quarters. For gatherings, much like here, there is one large cave at the entrance, and the Great River passes close enough. Life will not be as easy there as it is here, with the Mother Stream passing through Kthama's lower level. But it will be serviceable. The hardest part will be deciding who stays and who leaves."

"Will the males and females be separated as they are here? Is there enough room?"

"There will not be separate entrances as far as I can tell. But within the recesses of the system, yes, they can be separate to a point."

That will be a big change, thought E'ranale. Hopefully, by then, Moc'Tor's directive for males and females to mate selectively would have taken hold, if that is what he decides we should do. She wondered if her mate had thought that through any further. In the next moment, she knew he had.

"E'ranale, do you know if Ushca and Ny'on favor any of the other males?"

E'ranale cocked her head, "You are asking if they have a preference for a mate other than you?"

"Yes, I am asking that."

E'ranale was not sure how to respond. She decided she should answer carefully, not wanting to hurt Moc'Tor's pride if that were possible. "I do know that Ushca favors someone."

"Who? Which male?"

E'ranale sighed and stepped into it. "Straf'Tor."

"My brother?"

"Yes." She sighed again.

Moc'Tor looked off into the distance. E'ranale surmised that he realized this might not be as easy as he had thought.

"Hmmph," he said, then continued. "Have they mated? As far as I know, Straf'Tor favors Toniss."

"I do not know if they have mated. I believe they would think it disloyal to you, Moc'Tor, even though there is no prohibition against it."

E'ranale felt a twinge of jealousy that it bothered Moc'Tor if his Second Choice was interested in another male.

Moc'Tor ran his hand through his crown.

"What about Toniss?"

"Toniss mates with Straf'Tor because he chooses her. But she does not prefer him."

"This is getting complicated."

"It probably seems so to you, and I mean no disrespect. But you rightly do not spend as much time with the females as I do. I believe there would be less strife than you think. Given a chance, I believe that your brother and Ushca would choose to be together. I see them stealing glances at every opportunity."

"I am glad you know all this, but thinking about it makes my head hurt."

E'ranale stopped and turned to face Moc'Tor. She reached over with both hands and grabbed fistfuls of the thick hair behind his hips, pulling him to her.

"Then do not think about it."

Moc'Tor recognized her invitation and immediately fell to taking advantage of the opportunity. Obstructed by a fallen log was a small clearing to their left, and he broke from her long enough to heave it out of the way, opening up a secluded nook. Kicking aside the rocks and leaves, he laid her down on the soft soil and took her readily, then and there. Knowing she was already seeded and he would not be adding further to the overpopulation allowed Moc'Tor fully to surrender himself to the relief she offered. For a moment at least, he was freed of the burdens of leadership, lost in the pleasure of claiming his First Choice.

Thousands of years later, Khon'Tor impatiently waited for the female he loved to return to his bed. He had not liked hearing that his son, Akar'Tor, was looking her over. Whatever the young male's interest in her, Khon'Tor would not tolerate it. His entire life had turned around when he took Tehya as his mate. And he was not going to let anything threaten to destroy the peace and happiness he had found with her. He tensely waited until she came back to their Quarters; only when she was back, lying beside him, did he let himself surrender to the rest his body still so badly needed.

Acaraho handled all the plans for the return of the High Council, regularly keeping Khon'Tor updated. He had received confirmation that all the Leaders,

Healers, and Helpers would be coming from as far away as the Great Pines and the High Red Rocks. As before, guards were in place along the route. Though the Waschini threat had not materialized as they feared, they still could not risk the discovery of those who had to travel overground.

Mapiya and the females had worked with Acaraho and his males as before to shore up supplies and prepare living quarters. Nadiwani had finally returned to the High Rocks and Ithua to her village. Khon'Tor's strength returned, and he and Nootau were both recovered by the time the People of the High Rocks were to receive their guests. Adia often wondered if Khon'Tor or Nootau would be among those left sterile by the illness. Only time would tell.

Khon'Tor, Tehya, Acaraho, Adia, Nadiwani, Mapiya, and Awan sat in their planning room, going over last-minute details. Khon'Tor found himself wishing that Oh'Dar was there. He had been a great help before he left. The Leader knew Adia also wished he was there, though for different reasons. Having no idea of the young male's whereabouts, Khon'Tor knew of no way to contact him.

"At what point do you want Haan to return, Khon'Tor?" asked Acaraho.

"I expect that this meeting will spread out over many days, perhaps longer. Though we have no idea what the others will report, there are enough communities for it to last well past the length of the Ashwea Awhidi. No doubt, Haan's appearance will dominate the stage. I would like to hear from the other communities before everyone's attention is focused on his presence."

Acaraho spoke again. "Since I have no way of knowing how long it will take for the tree break to be noticed, I believe we have to initiate contact when all the High Council members are assembled, before the meetings begin."

"I will go with you, Acaraho, when it is time to signal for Haan," volunteered Adia.

"Very well," said Khon'Tor.

Kurak'Kahn, the Overseer, was the first member to arrive. Once he was settled in, Acaraho and Adia set out to make the tree break to signal for Haan's return.

"You must have had another reason for coming with me, other than enjoying my company, Adia?" Acaraho asked his mate as they walked.

Adia smiled. "I do enjoy your company; it is true. But yes, I would like to see if I feel the same presence there as I did before.

Acaraho wrapped his fingers around hers and shortened his stride to match her pace as they continued on.

As they neared the end of the valley where the tree breaks were, Adia felt the same presence as before. This time, the hair on the back of her neck stood up. They were most definitely being watched.

Acaraho felt it too, and it raised his confidence that their message would be delivered to Haan in short order.

He did as Haan had instructed, taking the tears and pulling them lower. They took a moment to look around and listen to the wind rustling through the trees before returning to Kthama.

Akule once again found himself at the Leader's Quarters during personal hours. It was becoming a curse. *Why are these things always happening on my watch?* he asked under his breath, as he once again interrupted Khon'Tor's private time.

Khon'Tor left Tehya's side and responded to the unwelcome intrusion. As he went to the door, he saw the irony of Akule's presence there once more.

"This is becoming a bad habit of yours, Akule. What is it now?"

"We have a visitor. You have a visitor. Someone asking for asylum, or something."

Khon'Tor sighed and shook his head.

"Is this someone we know, Akule? What is going on?"

"It is your son."

Khon'Tor immediately thought of Nootau but luckily stopped himself in time. "My *son*?"

"Akar'Tor. Your son by Hakani. He is here."

Khon'Tor released an epithet, *"Quat Rok!"* Then he asked,

"Where exactly is *here*?"

"He is in your meeting room. I did not know where else to take him."

Khon'Tor sighed. *Lucky for you, Akule. Of all the times I have considered killing you for what you know about that night with Adia, this time I might have followed through had you brought him here to my quarters, near Tehya. I do regret ever allowing that PetaQ in here.*

"I will go to him, Akule."

"Yes, Adoeete."

"You were wise not to bring him here. Never bring him here. Ever. I do not want him anywhere near Tehya, here *or elsewhere*. Is that clear?"

"Yes, Khon'Tor. Perfectly."

"Akule. If you make a mistake in this, I promise you will pay for it with your life."

Khon'Tor stepped back inside to Tehya. "I have to leave for a while; wait for me here. Under no circumstances leave our quarters."

"What is it? You are scaring me."

"If it means you will stay here as I ordered, then it is good that you are frightened."

Tehya frowned at the return of his stern approach toward her. "I do not have to be frightened in order to obey you, Khon'Tor."

"Good; I am glad to hear that. Stay here, nevertheless. Understood?" he snapped.

"Yes, Adoeete."

Khon'Tor turned and left with Akule. About halfway down the corridor, he stopped. "No. Go back and stand guard by the door. I can handle Akar myself."

Akule did as he was told. Nothing was as important to Khon'Tor as Tehya.

Khon'Tor entered the meeting room, and Akar'Tor turned to face him. "Akar, I was not expecting to see you alone. Is your father with you?"

"*You* are my father. But to answer your question, no Haan is not."

"Is he coming? The last thing I remember him saying is that he might bring you back for the High Council meeting."

"Yes, I know."

"Then why are you here?"

"Just as I said. You are my father."

Insolent Soltark. Khon'Tor was already tired of this game. "What is it you want, Akar? Tell me now, and be brief."

"I am here to be your son. I am claiming my place as the heir to your leadership of the People of the High Rocks."

Khon'Tor frowned hard in disbelief at Akar'Tor's gall. "You know nothing about us. You know nothing about our culture. You are my son in name only; you have been raised among the Sarnonn. You might be fit to lead them as part of Haan's culture, but you are not fit to lead the People."

"Then you will teach me. It is my right, and I am claiming it."

Impossible. Just like his mother. This is the last thing I need. Akar here? Around Tehya? Not going to happen.

"Sit down," ordered Khon'Tor, realizing this was going to take a while. He waited a moment for the young male to sit. When he did not, Khon'Tor placed a heavy hand on Akar's shoulder and shoved him down—*hard*.

"I said, sit. One who wants authority for himself must honor it in another. That is your first lesson."

Akar's eyes darkened, but he stayed put.

"Now, who has put this idea in your head? Was it your mother? Hakani?"

"She had nothing to do with it."

Oh, I doubt that very much. "She must have had something to do with it, or how would you know even to ask such a thing?"

"My mother has told me some things about my position as your son, it is true. But it was not her idea for me to come here. She has no idea I came. Neither does Haan."

Khon'Tor ran his hand through the silver crown of his hair. *Great. More good news. That means Hakani might end up here looking for him. She had better not.*

"What is it you hope to accomplish? Are you looking for a way to join us, be one of us? To do that, you do not need to force a claim you cannot even understand. We accepted Oh'Dar, the Waschini. The People of the High Rocks will accept you, too."

"But I do not just want to be part of the People. I want to lead."

"It is not that simple, Akar. Leadership is not as simple as sharing a bloodline."

"Why not? You have no other heir."

Not exactly true, thought Khon'Tor as Nootau again sprang to mind. *But for all intents and purposes, Akar is right.* A cold chill ran through him, remembering the sickness that had finally left his body. *And if I cannot seed Tehya—the 'Tor line will die with me.*

"No doubt one or both of your parents will be along shortly once they figure out you are gone. We can all sit down and discuss it at that time. For now, I am going to take you to a living space. I want you to stay there until morning. Is that clear?"

Akar'Tor nodded, not taking his eyes off Khon'Tor.

"Are you hungry? Do you need something to eat?"

The young male shook his head, no.

"Alright, then. Follow me. I will get you settled in, and we will discuss this in the morning. When you arise, go to the general meal area immediately. Go nowhere else. Once there, find a seat and stay until I find you. Is that clear?"

Khon'Tor stood up and waited for Akar'Tor to also come to his feet. Then he led this younger version of himself back into the Great Chamber, looking out for one of Acaraho's guards. Spotting First Guard Awan, the Leader signaled him over.

"Please escort Akar to one of the empty sleeping areas. In the morning, at first light, have someone escort him to the meal area."

Awan nodded and turned to lead Akar'Tor away, but not before noting the cold look in Khon'Tor's eyes.

Acaraho came into the Great Chamber as they were leaving. "I saw you with Akar'Tor. What is going on, Khon'Tor?"

"Are you on duty?"

"No. I could not sleep and did not want to disturb Adia with my tossing and turning. Too much on my mind."

"He came here to claim his position as heir to my leadership."

Acaraho's eyes widened, and he shook his head. "Just like that?"

"Just like that."

"He came alone?"

"Yes, but we both know it will not be long until Hakani or Haan realize he is missing, and one or the other—or both—will show up. We are expecting Haan, but Hakani—"

"Let me find out where Awan has taken him. I am sure you would feel better with a guard or two outside his room."

Khon'Tor raised his eyebrows and thanked Acaraho. Everything had been so much easier since Adia had ended the war between the three of them.

Acaraho was a formidable opponent and far better for Khon'Tor to have as an ally.

"I asked Akule to stand guard outside my quarters."

"I will take care of that, too. Akule serves best as a watcher, not a guard. I will find others better trained to protect Tehya. I mean, there is no one better to protect her than you, but—"

"I know what you mean, Acaraho. Thank you."

"We had better get some rest now. We have some long days ahead of us."

The two males parted—Khon'Tor to return to his beloved Tehya and the High Protector to take care of placing the guards.

It was some time before Acaraho stretched out next to Adia. She stirred as his weight hit the sleeping mat, and she turned to cuddle up next to him.

"Where have you been?"

"I could not sleep. Too many details on my mind. By the way, Akar'Tor is here."

Adia propped herself up on one elbow. "That is it."

"That is *what*?"

"That feeling in the meadow. The one of feeling watched. The one that makes the hair on the back of my neck stand up. It was Akar'Tor. I felt it again very strongly about an hour ago; that must have been when he arrived. There is something—wrong there, Acaraho."

"What you are saying does not surprise me. I will make sure Tehya is well protected."

"Why is he here?"

"He wants to claim his position as heir to Khon'-Tor's leadership of the High Rocks."

Adia tried not to feel guilty, remembering the conversation she'd had with Akar'Tor about precisely that. *I hope I did not put that thought in his head.* She lay back down, and resting her head on Acaraho's shoulder, tried not to think about the trouble this would stir up.

Acaraho was awake early, tending to the arrival of the other Leaders and Healers as they trickled in. He was making chalk marks on the wall of the planning room to record who had already arrived. Before they could begin, they were still waiting on the Leaders and Healers from the People of the Great Pines.

On his way to check that Akar'Tor was still where he was supposed to be, Acaraho stopped to greet the High Council Overseer.

Despite what had occurred the last time they were here—or perhaps because of it—Kurak'Kahn greeted Acaraho with respect once again. Perhaps the time had healed the burn of Adia's words since she had told off the High Council, revoking her accu-

sation against Khon'Tor and taking all the power of
the matter forever out of their hands.

"Good Morning, Overseer. I trust you slept well?"

"Yes, Commander, thank you. I am anxious for us
to get started. Is everyone here now?"

"We are still waiting for Risik'Tar of the Great
Pines, and his companions. Everyone else is here and
settled. Many of them are already here for the
morning meal. Khon'Tor will address everyone
beforehand because of the curiosity your visit is
causing."

As if on cue, Khon'Tor entered with Tehya at his
side, two guards not far behind them. The Leader
scanned the room looking for one figure only. Not
seeing Akar'Tor, he sent one of Tehya's guards to
fetch the young upstart. *Will not follow simple directions, yet he thinks he is fit to lead.*

Khon'Tor led Tehya over to where Adia, Nadiwani, and the others in their circle were sitting.

"Good morning. May we join you?"

"Of course," Adia said, sliding over to make room
for Tehya and Khon'Tor to sit on her side of the rock
slab.

☾

Tehya slipped in next to Adia. Setting aside his
prohibition against public affection, Khon'Tor
straddled the slab, encircling Tehya between his
thighs, but still sitting where he could watch the

crowd. A smug, self-satisfied smile crossed his face as the huge Alpha male took pleasure in demonstrating his ownership of this tiny desirable female. Tehya instinctively leaned back into him and sighed as the tension left her body. She found his concern for her frightening, but as she relaxed, she realized how much stress he was carrying. The warmth of him against her back, the rise and fall of his chest as his warm breath hit her neck; both gave her more comfort than she had ever known. She snuggled back against him. Had he not been on high alert, the pressure would have aroused his desire for her. But she knew there was too much demanding his attention to give in to that right now.

Adia was talking, but Tehya was not paying attention because she was also now watching the room, waiting for the same thing Khon'Tor was waiting for —Akar'Tor's appearance. Before long, one of the female greeters led Risik'Tar of the Great Pines and his companions into the area and got them settled.

Now everyone was there as far as she knew, except for Akar'Tor. Mapiya joined them, bringing a selection of food for Khon'Tor and his mate. He raised his hand in thanks.

Mapiya set the items in front of Tehya, who looked away.

"You need to eat." Khon'Tor sounded tense.

"I am not hungry yet."

"Eat anyway," ordered Khon'Tor. "It is going to be

a long day, and I am going to be occupied. I cannot worry about whether or not you have eaten."

His bluntness embarrassed her and hurt her feelings.

He is always ordering me around now. Is he just stressing, or is this what Hakani warned me about? Is he starting to turn mean toward me? No, I will not let myself think like that. She hates him; she would say anything to drive a wedge between us. When this is over, he will become his gentle self again. I must understand the burden he carries as Leader, and not expect him always to mind how he speaks to me.

Tehya did as Khon'Tor had said and forced herself to eat what was set before her.

"I need to greet Risik'Tar of the Great Pines and the rest of the High Council, and then make a general announcement. Today, you must stay close to Nadiwani, Adia, or Mapiya, or go back to our quarters. Do you understand?" Khon'Tor whispered into her ear.

"Yes. I am sorry you are so worried; I will do as you say. I do not want to cause you any more stress, Adoeete."

He looked to make sure no one was watching and then inhaled the scent of her hair. Lavender and pine. He let out a long sigh before releasing her and rising.

The others at the table exchanged looks but said nothing as they watched him walk away. Adia reached over and patted Tehya's hand.

Khon'Tor approached Risik'Tar and the others. As he crossed the room, he signaled to one of the guards lined up along the wall to sound the Call to Assembly Horn.

"Good morning, Risik'Tar. Have you just arrived, or did you come in during the night?"

"Good morning, Khon'Tor. No, we have just arrived. It took a little longer than we thought."

"You must be tired. I am going to make an announcement, and then there will be a break before we meet for our discussion. You will have time to settle in before we assemble."

Risik'Tar turned toward a female who stood just beyond him. "This is Tapia, our Healer."

Khon'Tor greeted Tapia and nodded to Risik'Tar and the others just as the final Call to Assembly Horn sounded. The Leader made his way to the front of the room, doubtful that anyone was voluntarily missing the excitement. Except for Akar'Tor. *Of course.*

The Leader took his place on the speaking platform at the front of the room. As he raised his left hand, all eyes in the room became instantly focused on him alone.

Tehya looked Khon'Tor up and down. *I cannot believe he is my mate; he is magnificent.* Her insides curled, and she suddenly realized that she wanted to be alone with him—*now*.

"Good morning, everyone. This is an occasion of historic proportions for all our people. I am sure you are aware that we have been joined by the Leaders and Healers from all the People's communities. While I cannot reveal the subject of our meeting, rest assured that it is focused on the wellbeing of all our populations. Please join me in welcoming our guests. Once the High Council meeting is over, I will share with you something most beneficial. Your trust in us, your Leaders, is paramount to our being able to guide you through the challenges ahead as we further our understanding of Wrak-Ayya and the adjustments we must make—not only to survive but to continue to thrive as a people. Thank—" Khon'-Tor's eye was pulled to some motion in the back of the room.

Akar'Tor entered and started walking toward the front, just as the Leader was finishing his speech. Khon'Tor glared at him, daring him to step foot on the platform, but to no avail. Khon'Tor's eyes narrowed. *Not again.* Akar'Tor approached and abruptly took a place, standing right next to him.

A murmur rolled through the crowd.

"Oh, no," said Adia, just as Acaraho and two guards made a beeline to the front of the room.

Akar'Tor glanced at Khon'Tor. Ignoring the Leader's angry expression, he faced the gathering.

The High Council members stared at the two virtually identical figures on the platform. Khon'Tor could see the confusion on the Overseer's face as Kurak'Kahn struggled to understand what was happening and why there were two of him.

"I am Akar'Tor. As the son of Khon'Tor and Hakani, I claim my right as heir to his leadership."

Khon'Tor could not suppress the snarl on his lips as his fury flamed against Akar'Tor. "This is not appropriate, Akar," he growled.

"I am claiming my right. I want everyone to know," the young male replied.

At that moment, Acaraho and the two guards reached the front. Acaraho faced Akar'Tor, the guards flanking him.

"Come with me. *Now!*" ordered Acaraho.

Akar'Tor did not move.

"Either you come with me willingly, or I will drag you out of here myself," Acaraho snarled through clenched teeth.

Akar'Tor threw a searing look at Khon'Tor before leaving with the High Protector and his guards.

The murmur in the crowd now rose in fervor as Akar'Tor was led out of the room. Khon'Tor's eyes burned as he watched the upstart leave.

Tehya slid off the rock slab, and within seconds, was at her mate's side.

"Thank you, everyone," and Khon'Tor closed his speech, doing his best to hide his anger. "To our visitors, we hope you enjoy your stay. If there is anything you need, please ask me or anyone else."

Tehya slipped her hand into his and walked with him from the platform. Khon'Tor gritted his teeth and balled his other hand into a fist to control his rage. He let his mate lead him from the front of the room, grateful for her assistance but angry that it was necessary. In the past, he would have been furious at anyone thinking he needed to be rescued, but he was beyond addressing the crowd any further without betraying his rage against Akar'Tor.

"Stay with them," Khon'Tor told Tehya, back at Adia's table.

"Where are you going?"

"To kill Akar," he replied and then stormed off. Tehya decided he was just letting off steam—she hoped.

Khon'Tor passed Kurak'Kahn on the way out but said nothing. The Overseer turned to the others at his table and said, "Welcome to the High Rocks, where there is never a dull moment."

Storming into the closest room, where they had taken Akar'Tor, Khon'Tor pushed past Acaraho and the two guards. He grabbed the young offender by the throat, and still in forward motion, slammed him against the rock wall. Akar'Tor's hands went instinctively to Khon'Tor's, which were tightly wrapped around his neck.

Inches from his son's face, Khon'Tor snarled, revealing his sharp canines, as his eyes burned into those of the young male. "Offspring or not, I should kill you right here for your insolence."

Akar'Tor struggled, but despite their similar build, he did not have the muscles or training that Khon'Tor did—or the adrenaline-fueled rage that drove the Leader. "What gives you the right to interrupt me when I am addressing my own community? *Who do you think you are*?"

"I am your son, Khon'Tor. Like it or not," Akar'Tor managed to choke out.

"You may be a product of my seed, but you are *not my son*. You have not earned that title. You do not get to walk in here and claim a position at my side. It is not yours to claim; it is yours to earn and mine to grant. Do you *understand* that?"

Khon'Tor tightened his grip on Akar'Tor's throat, well aware that a little more pressure would crush his windpipe.

"I understand that you are as my mother said— arrogant, overbearing, cruel," Akar'Tor gasped, struggling for air.

"This is not cruelty, Akar. What your mother did to Adia was cruel. What she did to Adia's son Nootau was cruel. And some of what I did to Hakani was cruel. But *this* is not cruelty; this is what you have coming. I could easily have struck you down in front of everyone, and no one would have blamed me. Even *that* would not have been cruelty—that would have been justice. You behaved like a spoiled *PetaQ'*. You have done nothing to impress anyone with your so-called leadership abilities—quite the opposite."

Khon'Tor released his hold on Akar's neck and shoved him down to the hard floor, almost disappointed to see him remain there. He willed Akar'Tor to rise, defiant. Khon'Tor would have welcomed an excuse to beat him to a bloody pulp.

"That is what I should have done to you publicly, Akar. That is what you deserved for what you just did. You are definitely your mother's son, that is certain. Get him out of my sight," Khon'Tor then spat out.

Acaraho signaled, and the guards hoisted Akar'Tor off the floor, ignoring his coughing.

"When your *father* gets here," said Khon'Tor, referring to Haan, "we will see what *he* thinks of your immature stunt."

Acaraho approached Khon'Tor as the guards led Akar'Tor away. "We need to get back. Immediately."

"I cannot believe he did that. I only hope Haan will back me up." Khon'Tor ran his hand through his hair and tried to calm down. He was having flashbacks to the chaos and havoc that Hakani had caused years ago in front of the community over Oh'Dar.

"Well, we will not have to wait long to find out. Haan came in just as Akar'Tor was speaking."

"What? Haan is in there? In the room with *everyone?*"

Forgetting decorum, Khon'Tor and Acaraho raced back to the eating area to find the visitors frozen in silence and fear, and all eyes pinned on the giant Sarnonn standing just inside the entrance.

Khon'Tor immediately moved to stand next to Haan, who looked down and signed, *"Sorry."*

Feeling a wave of relief, Khon'Tor realized Haan must have witnessed Akar'Tor's stunt and agreed that his actions were out of line. Or else Haan was apologizing for his unexpected presence in a room full of startled Akassa. Either way, he wasn't angry, and that was most of all what Khon'Tor needed to know.

"Please, come with me," and Khon'Tor headed for the front of the room.

All heads turned to follow the Alpha as he and the mammoth hair-covered figure took their places on the speaking platform.

Adia still hadn't got over how unnerving Haan appeared on the surface. As large as he was, Khon'Tor looked like a youngster standing next to the Sarnonn. Haan's full, dark covering that blanketed his body, his deep-set dark eyes that stared back at the crowd, his massive shoulders that topped a barrel chest, and his thighs like tree trunks—all elicited fear in anyone at first sight. Even the sound of his deep-chested breathing could start hearts pounding.

Kurak'Kahn and the other High Council members leaned forward, waiting for Khon'Tor to speak.

"This is Haan, Leader of the Sassen, whom we call the Sarnonn. He has come to speak with the High Council." Khon'Tor turned to Haan and prayed to the Great Spirit that he would pick up the cue. He did.

"Greetings to you," Haan signed. "As Khon'Tor said, I am the Leader of the Sassen tribe. I come in peace and bring a hearty welcome to your people from mine. I apologize for my son's actions. I did not raise him to behave so."

If there was confusion before, it ran rampant now. Khon'Tor stepped in, not wanting to go into this with everyone and certainly not in this forum, but seeing no other choice.

"Those of you who are not part of Kthama may not know the story, so let me briefly explain. Many years ago, we believed my first mate Hakani had died from a fall to the Great River while seeded with my offspring. Hakani did not die as we thought, but was rescued by Haan and accepted into his community as his mate. The offspring that Hakani carried, by my seed, is Akar, who addressed you earlier. Haan accepted Akar as his son, who has therefore been raised as one of the Sarnonn all his life. I only recently learned of his existence, as well as that of Haan and his people. I know that is not enough to answer all your questions, but it is all I can share at the moment."

Khon'Tor took a step forward. "The most important point—and the one I want you to remember above everything else said this morning —is that there is peace between our people and Haan's. There is nothing to fear. Please welcome Haan and our other guests. Now, please excuse us. High Council members, ask any of the guards to escort you to the meeting area as soon as you are ready."

So much for a break.

Khon'Tor turned to Haan, and they stepped down from the stage.

Haan signed, "Please take me to Akar."

"Come with me." Khon'Tor led him from the Great Chamber, but not without first glancing at Tehya to see how she was doing. She nodded to him; she was alright.

The two Leaders passed down the corridor to the quarters occupied by Akar'Tor for his stay. They entered to find the younger version of Khon'Tor sitting with his face in his hands. He jumped up as he saw Haan enter.

Haan stood in the doorway, looking down at the offling he had raised as his own. He knew that Akar'Tor was struggling, but Haan could not let his feelings mitigate what needed to be done.

"Akar'Tor. You shame me."

Akar'Tor's mouth hung open, and he looked away.

"Father, please. Do not say that."

Khon'Tor noticed how different Akar's countenance was before Haan. *This hulking giant Sarnonn is his father. Not me. It is so obvious; why can Akar not see it for himself? Even I understand this. Siring someone is not the same as being their father.*

"How did I shame you? I was claiming what is mine. I thought that was what a Leader should do."

"A Leader does not claim a position to lead by arrogance. A Leader earns his place through years of proving that he is worthy of leading. A Leader is raised into his position through the community's faith in his abilities. Forcing yourself into a position you have not earned is not leadership. That dramatic show you put on was not leadership; it was rude and immature. You disrespected the greatest Leader of the People in front of his entire community as well as their High Council. You did nothing but prove the contrary—that you are in no way suited to lead. I thought I taught you better. But I have failed you somehow, and for that, I am very sorry."

Haan spoke in the language of the Sarnonn, but Khon'Tor understood enough by now. The giant had pretty severely admonished Akar'Tor for his actions.

Instead of railing against Haan, Akar'Tor crumbled. He rushed to Haan and pressed himself against the only father he had known. Khon'Tor thought he might have even seen the glint of tears in his eyes.

"Please do not say that, Father. Please."

Haan put his hand on Akar'Tor's shoulder but said nothing. He continued to stand erect and did not return Akar's embrace.

"I will leave you alone," said Khon'Tor. "Haan, there are guards outside the door, but they were put there to monitor Akar, not yourself. You are, of course, free to move about. When you are ready to join us, ask anyone where we are meeting. I do prefer Akar stay here for now until things calm down."

Haan nodded and glanced at the door, letting Khon'Tor know it was alright to leave, so he and Acaraho filtered out.

Once out of earshot, Khon'Tor turned to Acaraho. "Well, I can safely say the High Council now knows about Haan."

Acaraho smiled at the dark humor, relief allowing him to relax his shoulders since even Khon'Tor was able to joke about it.

"We had best get ready for the meeting," Acaraho said, placing a hand on Khon'Tor's shoulder.

Adia would be pleased if she could see what her forgiveness set in motion. The anger and the battles between the three of us are over. We are becoming the unified leadership of the People for which she always hoped.

"I am bringing Tehya to the High Council meeting."

"I doubt they will object, Khon'Tor. She is Third Rank, after all. And it is High Rocks which is the most deeply affected by the appearance of the Sarnonn."

"She stepped up today, Acaraho. She is proving her desire to undertake the other duties of her role as my mate. She needs to hear first-hand what the People are facing. And the High Council must expand. The Healers and Helpers have to be a permanent part moving forward. Perhaps even all the Third Rank. We are facing serious issues, and we need all the wisdom and different viewpoints we can get."

Acaraho nodded in agreement.

"I am going to fetch Tehya. I will be with you all shortly."

Khon'Tor panicked for a moment when he could not find Tehya in the common eating area he had just left.

"Where is she, Adia?"

"She left with the two guards. She said she was going to your quarters, and that I should tell you she is there."

Khon'Tor nodded and immediately left to find his mate.

He brushed past the two guards outside the Leader's Quarters and found Tehya there as promised. She turned as she heard him come in. Khon'Tor rushed over to her. He took her face in his hands and kissed her softly, then drew her toward him. As he circled his huge arms around her, he felt her melt into his embrace.

Not saying a word, Tehya pulled back and stretched up on her tiptoes to give him her own kiss. He leaned over to meet her lips, then again, more passionately. He welcomed her invitation and swept her up and carried her to their bed. He lay down next to her and pulled loose the ties of her wrappings. He wanted her more than he ever had before.

Khon'Tor kissed her neck and whispered her name. He lightly teased the tips of her exposed mounds and then gently drew one into his mouth and heard her sigh in pleasure. He ran his hands over the front of her, continuing to please her, tease her, then burying his face in her neck and inhaling deeply. He parted her thighs with his, readying his position to claim her, then slid his hands under her hips and pulled her close to him, placing himself hard against her. His desire for her swelled to full capacity as he felt her wet readiness for him.

"Tehya," he whispered as he pressed against her and kissed her again. She arched her back in response to his pressure at her opening. Being careful not to crush her, he slowly entered, as far as he dared. Each stroke rocked her tiny form beneath him. He took his time until he felt her tighten around him as pleasure rippled through her.

As her release waved over him, he held back his own pressing need to spend inside her. He wanted to own her a little while longer, feel her so small and delicate under him, knowing he was pleasing her just as she was pleasing him. He wanted it never to end. He loved her and realized he had never loved anyone before. He had thought he loved Adia, but he had lusted after her, was seduced by her beauty. He could see now how different it was with Tehya.

This was an overpowering drive to protect her,

claim her, *own* her, dominate her. His mind was filled with only her as he exploded, filling her with his seed. He felt her relax under him, thinking they were finished, but his need for her had not been satisfied. Within moments he had recovered and took her again, this time with a little more force. She yielded to him and moaned as he reminded her that she was his and his alone. The thought of anyone else touching Tehya filled him with rage as he pumped his last reserves deep within her.

Khon'Tor carefully rolled off and collapsed to her left. She immediately curled up against him and buried her face in his neck. She kissed his ear and told him she loved him and only him. And that nothing would ever change that.

"Promise me, Tehya."

"I promise, Adoeete."

Khon'Tor felt his heart lurch. Now that he had loosened the stranglehold of his will on himself, he realized how angry he had always been and how tightly he had reigned over everyone.

"Did I hurt you?" he asked.

"No. I mean, yes. It cannot be helped; you are so much larger than I am built. But it was still wonderful. And I think I may be adjusting some. I do not know how to explain it."

Khon'Tor pulled her closer and kissed the top of her head. He understood the female's need for both the splendor of the release and the satisfaction of the filling.

"There is no one in my heart but you, Tehya. There never will be. If I lost you, I would have nothing left to live for."

"You will never lose me, Adoeete. I am here to torture you for the rest of your life."

Khon'Tor chuckled and once again thanked the Great Spirit for giving him the treasure of this innocent, loving female currently wrapped around him—who seemed to adore him for reasons he would never understand.

"I do not know why you love me so, Tehya. But I am grateful for every moment that you do."

Tehya threw one leg over his waist. Khon'Tor felt himself respond to her open vulnerability, but he did not have time to take her a third time without having to rush away immediately afterward. And he had vowed never to mate her and leave her abruptly like that.

"I cannot wait to spend time with you again tonight—after this day is over. But now I need to leave, and I need you to come with me."

"Where to? I thought you were meeting with the High Council."

"I am. And you are coming with me. You need to be a part of this, Tehya. You are my mate and Third Rank. It is appropriate that you join us since this affects High Rocks at such a deep level. I believe the entire makeup of the High Council needs to be reconsidered."

Tehya nodded. "I need a few moments to clean up."

"No. Do not. I want my scent on you."

Tehya blushed. "But what if the other males can tell?"

"Oh, Saraste'. That is exactly the point."

Tehya blushed further but did as he said, gathering her wraps from the disarray of the sleeping area.

"Put on something else," he told her.

Her hand went to her mouth as she looked down in shame.

"If I walk in wearing something different—"

"Do not be ashamed, Tehya. They know that you are mine. I just want to make it clear in subtle ways."

"I am not sure that these fall under subtle ways, Adoeete."

"Even better," he said, slapping her playfully on her backside as she got up. Tehya stepped into the private area to dress, and despite his order, removed some of his presence from herself. When she came out, he was standing waiting for her.

"Did you defy me, Tehya?" he asked, looking down at her.

She turned away as guilt colored her cheeks.

"I had to, Khon'Tor. I could not go in there like that. But I did not remove all of you."

"Next time, Tehya, disagree with me if you will, but do not disobey me behind my back."

The sternness had returned to his voice, and

Tehya nodded silently in response. Khon'Tor dropped to his knees and pulled her forward, pressing his face into where he had just deposited his seed. He inhaled the warm scent of them both mixed together from between her legs. He felt her pull back in embarrassment and held her tighter, not ready to leave her delicious scent. Oh, there was so much more he wanted to do to pleasure her, but she was not ready. "You are mine, Tehya. Only mine. I will kill the male who dares even to *think* of touching you."

The Leaders, their Healers, and the Helpers they trusted enough to bring were assembled in the meeting room by the time Khon'Tor arrived with Tehya. First Guard Awan was stationed outside with a multitude of other guards—all out of earshot.

Where to start, he thought, seating Tehya next to Adia. He remained standing to speak, a smile on his lips as he noticed many of the males in the room looking at his mate. It angered him and excited him at the same time. *Stare all you want. But tonight it will be me she is underneath, moaning as I bring her to the splendor and fill her to overflowing with my seed.*

The Alpha in Khon'Tor made him enjoy having what no other could—and flaunting it. And such a rare jewel as Tehya, at that.

"I am glad that you all made it. Ordinarily, I

would know where to begin, but the morning's events have changed the tone of our meeting."

Kurak'Kahn was the first to speak up. "We understand, Khon'Tor. And as I am sure you can appreciate, we all have a thousand questions about Haan. Also, you have brought your mate to the meeting."

"Yes, Overseer. The High Council needs to expand. We are facing unprecedented times. Since Tehya is Third Rank, and much of what is going on affects High Rocks directly, I deemed it appropriate. Now, as for Haan, he will be joining us shortly. While we await him, let me try to answer some of your questions, and before we end today, I want a report from each community—whether or not you have encountered any other settlements of the People or of the Sarnonn."

Kurak'Kahn scowled openly, but Khon'Tor received no verbal response indicating he should not proceed; he continued to own the floor.

"As you heard me explain earlier, my first mate was believed to have died, taking my unborn offspring with her. Earlier this year, we learned that was not true when she and Haan showed up here at Kthama. Your directive last year, Kurak'Kahn, to scout the areas looking for other communities— coupled with some other circumstances I will explain in a moment—provided them a timely opportunity to make contact. I trust I do not have to explain my shock at finding Hakani alive and my son with her."

Khon'Tor moved across the room. He spotted Urilla Wuti in the crowd seated with her Alpha, Harak'Sar, as well as the familiar face of Lesharo'Mok from Adia's original community. Many of the faces he did not recognize but assumed they were the Healers and Helpers who had accompanied their Leaders to the meeting. From the Leaders whom he had faced when Adia brought her accusation against him, and he had admitted his crime against her, he could feel newfound distrust and disdain.

"As you now know, Hakani did not die; Haan found her. He took her into his community and brought her back to health, along with the offspring, Akar'Tor. There they remained until recently."

Khon'Tor saw glances exchanged when he mentioned Haan had a community. "My offspring has been raised as one of the Sarnonn. He fell ill, and it was only his sickness and Hakani's condition that brought them to us. Hakani was carrying Haan's offspring when she came to our Healer, Adia, for help."

Conversation started up but was immediately silenced by Kurak'Kahn.

"Continue, Khon'Tor."

"Because a male Sarnonn had mated a female of our own, the offspring was too large for the mother and could not be allowed to go full term. Our Healers induced labor, and luckily the offspring survived. Then they returned to their community, but not before sharing information with our High Protector, Acaraho, that I knew would be of interest to you."

Khon'Tor turned to Acaraho, giving him the floor.

"Haan has information about the Wrak-Ayya, which changes our understanding of what happened," Acaraho said. "We invited him here to share his knowledge with you, especially considering the challenges we face, which you described the last time we met. According to Haan, the Wrak-Wavara was not between the Sarnonn and the Brothers. There was an earlier root which mated with the Brothers to produce us and the Sarnonn as we know them today. He called them the Mothoc."

Now not even Kurak'Kahn could bring the assembly immediately under control. Had they been ruthless rulers, they could have considered what Acaraho just shared to be heresy, and he would have been permanently silenced.

"Would you like to ask questions, or should Khon'Tor and I continue with our narrative?"

Kurak'Kahn spoke up. "You mentioned a recently born offspring; what became of it?"

Acaraho turned to look at his mate, Adia, the Healer, to answer.

Adia stood, "Her mother, Hakani, took her back to their community. She is fine as far as we know. She is clearly mixed, so there is no doubt that Hakani's story is true. She has a heavier coat and thicker features, but there is more evidence in her of the People than the Sarnonn. We have no way of knowing anything about her development in other areas. There was no possibility that the offspring could go to full term. Had Hakani not sought out our help and had the offspring delivered early, both she and the offspring would have perished. Breeding a male Sarnonn with any of our females is not a viable option."

"What about our males with one of their females?"

"Possibly, Overseer. But I doubt you would get any volunteers."

Kurak'Kahn nodded, having to concede her point. "When he spoke, I could almost understand him. He used Handspeak—so it appears we share a root language."

"Yes, combining Handspeak with speaking was an innovation of my Waschini offspring, Oh'Dar," Adia said. "I am sorry he is not here to meet with you. His help was instrumental in many regards. There is a common root language, which considering our shared past, is not too surprising. The speed at which they speak affects how much of their verbal talk we can understand."

Kurak'Kahn stood up to address the group, and Adia took her seat. "The last time we met, I asked each of you to send searchers out into your areas to see if you could discover any new communities of our people or any of the Sarnonn. Before we continue with this topic of Haan, does anyone else have anything to report?"

Harak'Sar of the Far High Hills stood. "We sent scouts out in all directions. None of them returned with anything to report."

By now, Kurak'Kahn had regained his composure and realized he had not formally opened the meeting. Neither had he explained any of the background to do with why the meeting was happening. He caught himself. "Before we continue, are there questions about why we are here? Not all of you were at the last meeting, though I am confident that you have been filled in on the situation by your Leaders who did attend." Kurak'Kahn scanned the group to see only nodding heads.

"Very well then, when Haan arrives, I will do a brief recap for him. Khon'Tor, will he understand us if we combine it with Handspeak as he did?"

Adia stood, "May I answer?"

Khon'Tor nodded.

"You will find his Handspeak to be rudimentary. I believe it has to do with a lesser level of dexterity due to his larger hands. Our hands are more delicate, and we have more motor control. In the beginning, I wrongly associated his use of baser words to be a reflection of his intelligence. I caution you not to make the same mistake. If Haan is representative, then the Sarnonn are just as intelligent as we are. Only in a larger package, to understate it."

Kurak'Kahn watched Adia as she spoke, remembering her scathing admonishment of him and the High Council the last time they were here. He had been angry with her and Khon'Tor for a long time thereafter. And he had still not forgotten her insolence in how she had addressed them—but neither had he forgotten the truth of what she had said. *She has a fire in her, and nothing we have done to her has put it out. As much as we have wronged her, she is still here in the fight with us. She has just shared that she underestimated Haan's intelligence based on his manual dexterity. I wonder if I have not made the same mistake and underestimated our females along the same lines.*

I am glad that we lifted the restriction against the pairing of Healers and Helpers. I hope she and Acaraho have found happiness despite our inexcusable misjudgment of them both.

Kurak'Kahn returned to the moment and felt Urilla Wuti staring at him. *Now there is another powerful female. She spent a great deal of time here with Adia while she was with offspring, and it was she who whisked the female offspring away from our knowledge. You can almost feel how connected she and Adia are. I wonder if the Healer community has its own secrets, just as do we of the High Council?*

Adia finished speaking as Haan entered the room. As before, all heads turned his way. Khon'Tor motioned for Haan to join him at the front. Having declined

Khon'Tor's offer to bring in a boulder that would support his weight so he could sit, Haan sat propped against the wall. No one moved, unsure what should happen next.

Khon'Tor retook the floor. "Thank you for coming." He turned to the others, "This is Haan. He is the Leader of the Sarnonn of Kayerm." There was silence through which the others nodded; it was a slow, reverent acknowledgment.

Khon'Tor turned back to Haan. "This is a meeting of the Leaders and Healers of the People's communities from across the land. We have come together to discuss a problem that we are all facing. We are hoping the information you share with us will help us solve our difficulties—which are serious. And we hope that we can be of some help to you in return. My wish is that this should be the beginning of a long and mutually satisfying relationship," Khon'Tor said.

"This is Kurak'Kahn. He is the Leader, the Overseer, or Adik'Tar of the High Council. Everyone else is either an Adik'Tar as I am or a Healer as is Adia," he continued, "except for Yuma'qia and Bidzel, who are knowledge keepers and work directly with the High Council."

"Until you showed up, Haan, we were not sure if there were any Sarnonn left—Sassen, as you call yourselves. We believed that your people and the Others, whom we call the Brothers, interbred to produce our kind, and any of you who were left would be in some far, remote region. But you explained that it was not your people who bred with the Others."

The group suppressed a gasp as Haan moved to stand at the front of the crowd. Even Khon'Tor felt intimidated by the giant's size and structure.

"I will now speak to you as equals," the huge Sarnonn said. "First, know that I come in peace. I see your fear. You are afraid of me—of us. You have no need to be afraid; we mean you no harm. My people have always been prevented from making contact with yours. Contact with you is forbidden to us, which is why you do not see us. But we have always been here."

The group breathed a collective sigh of relief. Once again, Kurak'Kahn was struck by the power of plain truth. They *were* afraid of him. Hearing him state it out loud was freeing.

"Many ages ago, there were no Sassen, no Akassa. Only the Mothoc and the Others. There was little contact between them, but the Mothoc protected and watched over the Others. The Mothoc are the Fathers-Of-Us-All. But they had no self-control and mated with the females freely. Too many offling were born, then the Great Spirit sent a sickness to the Mothoc as punishment for their lack of control, and many males died. So the Mothoc Leader gave the females the power to choose the males they preferred, and mating was limited to that one male of the female's choice. There was no more mating of females without their consent. The males were angry, and division and an uprising occurred."

Heads turned when Haan said *no mating without consent.* Khon'Tor uncomfortably shifted where he sat, pricked by confusing memories.

Kurak'Kahn himself wondered, *Was this the beginning of the First Laws? Never Without Consent? The Sarnonn forbidden to contact us? No Contact With Outsiders?*

Total silence fell across the room, despite the thousand questions in their minds—questions to which the full answers lay buried thousands of years in the past.

CHAPTER 5

Work to make the new location more habitable continued. Moc'Tor's crews went out in series, each spending several days there before coming back for more supplies. Females whitewashed some of the interiors to provide more light in the inner recesses, though the guards and sentries' night vision made much of it unnecessary. Moc'Tor named the new location Kayerm.

He, Drit the Fixer, and First Guard Dochrohan were enjoying Moc'Tor's favorite leisure occupation— sitting in front of a pleasing fire on a starry night. Moc'Tor was still struggling with implementing his idea that the males should mate with only one female. As if that part were not hard enough, getting the males to accept the second part—letting the females choose them—seemed even more of an impossibility. He poked at the fire with a stick as Oragur joined them.

"Moc'Tor, I am getting alarmed," Oragur said. "More are getting sick. I am not sure what to think of it, and nothing I do is helping." He paused. "Rathic returned to the Great Spirit today."

Moc'Tor put down the stick. "Rathic is gone?"

"Yes."

"He was one of our Elders, but still— And my father?"

"So far, he has not come down with it."

Moc'Tor sighed. He needed to spend more time with his father; he knew it. Though Sorak'Tor had handed over the leadership ages ago to help mentor and guide him through being a new Leader, the Guardian was not ready to lose his father. "How many of us have it now?" he asked.

"Almost half. It is worse in the males than the females, and I fear it is a punishment from the Great Spirit."

"For what?"

"For what you told us some time ago. That we were being irresponsible with our mating."

"Why do you think that?"

"Because it is affecting the male's seed packs. Not all, but in many of them, the seed packs are painfully swollen. To try and limit the spreading, we have placed all the sick in one of the lower rooms, but it seems to have no effect. But it would not if it is retribution—"

Moc'Tor had lived long enough that he was not sure he believed in such punishments from the Great Spirit. Still, even a loving father corrected his offling. "Keep me informed, Oragur."

He turned to his first guard. "Dochrohan, send a sentry up the Mother Stream to the other communities and see if they are also affected by this."

Over the next few weeks, Moc'Tor watched helplessly as a fourth of the males returned to the Great Spirit, and it was not restricted to those in their senior and twilight years. A dark pall hung over Kthama. Eventually, the sickness tapered off, but anguish remained.

Moc'Tor lay with E'ranale in the privacy of the Leader's Quarters, his worry drawing him to her. "I need to address the community. What is left of us, that is."

"There is nothing anyone could do, Moc'Tor."

"Oragur says it is a punishment from the Great Spirit."

"But you do not believe that."

"I do not know what I believe anymore. I have lived a long time, E'ranale, and in the end I have more questions than answers. Who is to say?"

"I can see why Oragur would believe it; he is the

Healer for one thing, and it did come after you had admonished the community for overbreeding. Except, the sentries said it is impacting all the communities up the Mother Stream."

E'ranale was starting to show, her waist thickening and her breasts enlarging. It was noticeable even under her thick hair. Moc'Tor rested his hand on her expanding belly.

"Since we have been talking about it, I believe more and more that we males need to control ourselves. Even despite our losses." Moc'Tor sighed. "I must address the community. It is time."

The next morning, he called an assembly. In contrast to when he had last spoken with them, the Great Chamber was not packed with bodies side-by-side. It was a sobering demonstration of their depleted numbers.

Moc'Tor moved to the front and looked out into a crowd of dark, somber faces. The females were clearly in mourning with lowered eyes and slumped shoulders. Angry scowls and clenched jaws prevailed among the males able to attend.

"I remember that the last time I stood before you, my message was one of concern for our overcrowding and our lack of self-control in our mating. As I look out now and see our depleted numbers, I am deeply saddened and somewhat ashamed.

"Oragur believes that this sickness is a punishment from the Great Spirit for being disrespectful of the bounty that was given us. For eons, our people have been blessed to live here in a land rich with supply. But that does not give us the right to squander what we have been given by overbreeding. So perhaps Oragur is right."

Someone shouted from the crowd, "You believe this is a punishment?"

"I believe it is possible."

"If we are being punished, what are we to do now?" called out another voice.

"If Oragur is right, then we need to change our ways while there is still time. By reducing our numbers, perhaps the Great Spirit is giving us a second chance. But if we do not change, then we invite further correction."

"But what about finding Kayerm? Is that not a blessing?"

"Yes. It truly was—and is. I do not have all the answers; perhaps Kayerm is not a blessing for this time but for a time yet to come. At any rate, there is now no need to split what is left of us. We have already ceased work there and closed off the entrance."

Moc'Tor stood silently and let them speak among themselves. He spotted Oragur in the crowd and motioned for the Healer to join him at the front.

"Oragur, are we being punished?" called out someone else.

Oragur made it clear that he had no doubts. "We are being corrected. We have been wasteful and let our numbers increase past that which even this great abundance could bear. Now we have suffered the consequences of our folly. Why else would the Great Spirit inflict a sickness that so targeted the source of our own demise? You have seen for yourselves the effects on the males who became sick and did not fully recover. Whether we listen or not will decree what happens to us next. Earlier, this room was packed to capacity; now there is but a portion of us left."

Moc'Tor did not completely agree with Oragur, but he saw the opening he needed and took full advantage of it. "Whether it is because we have been punished, or that the sickness is a result of our own foolishness, we have to change our ways. It will not be easy, but neither was what we have recently been through."

His Leader's Staff firmly in hand, Moc'Tor took a deep breath before continuing. "It is time for change. We males have had our way since the Great Spirit formed us from the dust of these walls. We now see where that has gotten us. We can no longer breed at will like the animals of the forest. We must be more than that because our future depends on it. From now on, the females will be the ones to choose whose seed to accept."

A gasp rolled through the crowd. The females stared at each other in amazement.

"Furthermore, the females will choose one male with whom to mate for the rest of both their lives. That is it. It will be the female's choice of who and how often. The males have had control for too long. Now it is time to let our females have their way."

"Are you sick yourself, Moc'Tor? You want us to wait for them to decide to mate? And let them choose who with?" asked a male named Norcab.

Moc'Tor had known there would be resistance and anticipated that it would start with Norcab. The Guardian stood taller, took a confident step forward, and stared down at the angry male. "Do you have another solution? You see where we are. If Oragur is right, our numbers have been reduced because of our inability to control ourselves. As I said, mating at will is beneath us; we must be better than that. I will give the females five nights to select their mates. Once this has happened, I expect you to honor their selection. If a female does not wish to pick a mate, that is also acceptable. Females are not to be taken without their consent. Not any more. Never again."

"I have never forced myself on any of them. Neither have any of the other males!" Norcab challenged the Leader.

"Have you not? Perhaps not physically forced, but have you ever considered whether the female you selected wanted to accept you into herself? Let alone to be seeded by you? They have given in because it was expected of them. Since we failed at treating them as equals, they are now elevated above us.

Anyone who does not agree with the new order is welcome to leave—now."

Moc'Tor's answer was a bedlam of voices. The females looked worried. The Guardian glanced at E'ranale and beckoned for her to join him. She frowned and remained where she was.

He motioned again, and this time she complied. Tentatively making her way through the crowd, E'ranale joined Moc'Tor on the platform. Then she suddenly realized that he wanted her to take the lead in following his order.

"People of Kthama."

The room silenced immediately at the unfamiliar voice—a female voice—speaking from the place of leadership where only males had ever stood.

"You have known me as Moc'Tor's First Choice. Now it is my choice as to whom I want to mate."

Utter. Abject. Silence.

For a moment, Moc'Tor actually felt afraid she was not going to choose him.

"I choose Moc'Tor," E'ranale whispered. Then, more loudly, she said, "I have always chosen Moc'-Tor." She placed her hand in his, then turned back to the crowd. "I have exercised my right to choose. Females, I urge you to consider well and choose wisely for yourselves. We are fortunate to have a Leader who seeks wisdom and understanding. Through adversity, great change has come; Moc'Tor has given us a position of equality, even reverence.

My prayer is that we live up to the mantle that has been placed upon our shoulders."

All eyes followed E'ranale as she led Moc'Tor from the stage. He squeezed her hand as they left and murmured just loud enough that only she could hear. "Perfect."

The couple moved to the back of the room and watched the outcome of their display. Oragur stayed near the front and answered questions as some of the audience pressed forward.

"I need to be with the females tonight, Moc'Tor."

"I understand. Though now that you have freely chosen me, I regret that we cannot spend our first night together."

"I will make it up to you, I promise."

"Go and be with them. I agree; they need your leadership now, E'ranale. I have done all I can."

She took her leave of Moc'Tor and went into the crowd. After gathering the females, she led them to the meeting cavern in their own cave system, where she could hear their concerns without the males being present.

❂

E'ranale had already prepared the females for what she believed was coming, so the idea of choosing who they wished to mate with was not a total surprise. The development was a boon for them, but still, the idea was not met without resistance.

Moc'Tor's former Second Choice, Ushca, spoke first. "The males are not going to accept this."

"They have little choice, Ushca. Moc'Tor has handed us the power to receive who we wish, and it is ours to accept or to give up. None of us has been pleased with the way things were."

"But I do not know how to choose," Ushca said.

"I think you do." E'ranale spoke gently. "What is really holding you back?"

"What if I choose someone who does not want me?"

"Doubtful. I have seen how he looks at you," said E'ranale.

Ushca lowered her eyes, thinking of her long-burning desire for Moc'Tor's brother, Straf'Tor.

"Moc'Tor and I discussed this at length," E'ranale continued. "This is the way it must be. If left to the males, we will only continue to have too many offling; you know this is true. When one female is seeded, the male goes on to the next even if she does not wish to be mated."

"We are not disagreeing with you, E'ranale. We just have no idea how to choose," said Toniss.

"You do not know how to choose, or you do not know who to choose? There is a difference."

The females exchanged glances and shifted uncomfortably.

"That is a good question," said Toniss after a moment. "Given the choice—"

The other females waited for her answer. They

knew Ushca favored Straf'Tor, but that he frequently chose Toniss. Ushca and Straf'Tor stayed away from each other, but only because Ushca was Moc'Tor's Second Choice.

"—I would not choose Straf'Tor."

Ushca frowned, "You would not choose Straf'Tor?"

"No. I am not sure why he even chooses me. Our mating is ritual and uninspired because he seems to burn for you, Ushca. Sometimes, I feel he is thinking of you when he is mounting me."

Ushca felt as if a fire had been lit within her at the thought that Straf'Tor might desire her as she did him.

"Well, this seems to be working out," E'ranale said. "Is it going to work out perfectly for each of us? No. But it is far from perfect the way it is now. We have been given power, and we have to try it. If you do not wish to choose now, do not. Wait until you know."

E'ranale let the females chatter among themselves for a few moments. Another question surfaced.

"If I know who I want, how do I know if he wants me?"

E'ranale now realized how truly out of balance the situation between the genders had become. And when things tilted too far, the Great Spirit made a correction. She leaned toward Oragur's interpretation that this was indeed a punishment from the

Great Spirit in an attempt to set things right. But it was sad that the females knew little about how to entice a male because the choice had always been made for them.

E'ranale answered, "Now that the males know they cannot mate any of us whenever they want, they are also going to be more selective. It is very simple. It is not so much choosing as offering. If you offer yourself to him and he does not move forward, then you have your answer."

"That makes it easier, E'ranale. Thank you."

"You do not have to be blatant about it. Brush up against him. Look at him, stare at him if you need to. Smile. Go slow. Believe me, he will be looking for the invitation. Just make sure he is the one you want before you make a move, as the odds are that unless he has a connection with another female, whoever you pick will accept you. Realize it is also hard for them."

The tension was easing, and E'ranale was exhausted. "Think about it for a while. There is no need to rush; we have five nights, and the males need time to adjust just as we do. Now I need to sleep. Tomorrow we enter a new age of control over whose seed we allow to be planted within us. A new age of choice."

Back in Kthama proper, Moc'Tor was dealing with the males, who were not taking the news as well as the females.

"Our numbers have been reduced, Moc'Tor. Why is this now even necessary?" asked one of the larger males.

"Trasik, if Oragur is right, it was a serious correction from the Great Spirit. If we do not heed this one, who knows how much worse the next correction might be?" said Moc'Tor. "I am not willing to take the risk."

"This is krellshar!"

"What exactly is bothering you about it, Trasik?" asked the Guardian.

"I no longer have the choice."

Moc'Tor scoffed. "I know your tastes, Trasik. You mated indiscriminately with anyone and everyone. You have never been selective to begin with, so what does it matter who chooses you? I doubt it is your loss of choice that you are complaining about. I suspect it is the control."

"Exactly. Now you have given them all the power," Trasik responded.

"They should have had it anyway. It does not mean you cannot approach them. But if you do, and one female accepts you, then you must limit yourself to her. It is very simple. One is the same to you as the other; I do not see your problem."

"We do not all feel that way, Moc'Tor," another voice spoke up.

Moc'Tor did not catch who had spoken, but he replied firmly. "I know this to be true. Some of you have been more selective in who you mated. If you admit it, many of you have your preferences."

It was time for Straf'Tor to come forward. "Moc'-Tor, E'ranale has chosen you. Are you to be content with mating only her?"

"I have been content for a long time, Straf. I seldom mated Ushca or Ny'on."

"What about you, Straf? Will you choose Toniss?" asked Trak, an alpha male of proportions equal to those of the huge Straf'Tor.

"I no longer get to choose; have you not been listening to my brother's words?" growled Straf'Tor in reply.

"You have mounted her in the past!"

"As have you! Not that who I have mounted is any of your business."

"I am making it my business. Do you want Toniss?"

When Straf'Tor did not answer, Trak stepped forward and snarled, "It is a simple question, Straf. Even a PetaQ such as you should be able to understand it. Answer me."

Tension flared as the two giants squared off. Moc'Tor had expected this, though not from his brother.

Straf'Tor pushed Trak in the chest, knocking him off-center. Trak lunged in return and succeeded in knocking his opponent to the ground. Dust flew as each struggled to gain a stronghold over the other, rolling into rock slab tables and benches as they fought. Trak pinned Straf'Tor by his shoulders, but Straf'Tor wrapped his huge muscled legs around Trak's midsection and flipped him over.

Now lying on his back, Trak snarled and snapped at Straf'Tor, trying to land teeth in flesh, but he was straddled with both shoulders pressed to the ground. Pieces of rock from broken benches dug painfully into his back. Straf'Tor chose his moment and lunged down, canines revealed. If he now pressed his advantage, he would tear open the main artery and Trak would quickly bleed to death. But it was enough that Straf'Tor had won the fight; he did not need to kill his adversary. Instead, he pressed his teeth into the meat of Trak's shoulder, and blood trickled from the gash.

Straf'Tor had drawn first blood, and accepting his defeat, Trak surrendered. Straf'Tor resisted his impulse to tear out Trak's throat anyway, instead giving him a final shove into the ground before releasing him and standing up. Trak rose, and glaring at Straf'Tor, he circled away, a hand pressed against the wound on his shoulder. Straf'Tor kept his eyes locked on Trak while flipping over a table with one hand and shattering it to pieces, his final demonstration of dominance.

Moc'Tor and the others watched as the battle between the two robust males flared and ran its course. The Leader had allowed the fight, knowing that both males needed to discharge the sexual frustration triggered by his announcement and that aggression against each other was a natural outlet. He now stepped forward into the rubble of the battlefield and circled, eyeing the males one at a time.

"Go about your ways. I have made my decision, and any one of you who cannot comply must be gone by first light. We have more challenges ahead, and I will not tolerate your disobedience. You have had your way with whichever females you wanted. Accept that those days are gone forever; the females now have the right to choose. If you wish to approach one instead of waiting for her, do so. But you must be prepared to accept refusal. Anyone taking a female without her consent will be banished, or worse."

"You are weak, Moc'Tor. You have let the females take power!" called out Norcab as Moc'Tor turned to leave.

"Who is calling me weak, who himself shouts out from within the crowd like a coward?" Norcab had often challenged Moc'Tor's authority, and the Leader knew this was just one more way for him to do so.

"Who are you calling a coward?"

Moc'Tor stepped into the throng and pressed his chest hard into Norcab's, locking eyes as he did so. "I am not just calling you a coward. I am stating a fact."

Norcab roared, grabbing Moc'Tor by the shoulders and twisting as he swept a foot forward, trying to knock Moc'Tor's feet out from under him.

Moc'Tor was the alpha for a reason. He stepped back from the maneuver and Norcab had to bring his other leg back and plant it quickly or lose balance. As Norcab recovered his equilibrium, Moc'Tor brought up one knee squarely between his opponent's legs, and on contact, Norcab doubled over in agony.

While Norcab was still writhing in pain on the ground, Moc'Tor leaned over, and with one hand, threw him against the rock wall. Norcab slid down in a massive dark heap, still curled over and clutching his throbbing seed pack.

Moc'Tor looked down at the incapacitated male in front of him. He then turned and looked back at the others. "Anyone else?"

Met with nothing but silence, Moc'Tor left, knowing that those outbreaks were not the end of it. There would be more attacks and skirmishes, but as long as the males' aggression was discharged only against each other, he would allow it. Change came hard for the Mothoc.

For the next two days, the males and females remained pretty much separate, neither sure of what to do. On the third day, they started to mingle again.

Sitting on their own in the Great Chamber, E'ranale asked Moc'Tor how it was going with the males after his announcement.

"As to be expected. Two skirmishes. One between Straf' and Trak. The other between Norcab and me."

"Norcab dared challenge a Guardian? What was that about?"

"The usual. Norcab is always looking for a chance to challenge me. I kneed him pretty hard and slammed him against the wall. He will be licking his wounds for a while. At some point, I will have to kill him, or he will kill me. It will not go away."

E'ranale knew her mate was right. Norcab had always been an angry beast. The day would come when Moc'Tor would have to end him, or his influence might spread to others. "Do not wait too long, Moc'Tor. Our people need a strong Leader to get them through these difficult times. You are both the Leader and a Guardian, and it is not good for them to see your decisions challenged. Even if Norcab is not coming at you directly, he might be working against you in the background, stirring up an organized backlash."

"You are right. For too long, I have allowed it to go on unchecked. The next time Norcab challenges me, I will end him as publicly as possible."

They both sat silent for a while.

Moc'Tor broke their reflection. "The females?" he asked.

"Relieved, I think, though unsure of their role now. They will adjust. I suspect we will not have to wait long for your brother and Ushca to pair up."

Moc'Tor smiled. At least there would be some entertainment out of all this.

Ushca stood at the meal counter, looking over the food that had been assembled. The hair on her back pricked up, and she knew that Straf'Tor had entered the Great Chamber. She took a deep breath. It was the first time she would be seeing him since Moc'-Tor's announcement, and her heart pounded in her chest. She sensed his approach and feared she might pass out.

Straf'Tor stood behind Ushca, and she could feel the heat coming off his body. She did not dare look around and stood frozen like a wary deer. A quiet whimper escaped her lips, and she closed her eyes and swore under her breath.

Straf'Tor took a step closer; he was now directly behind Ushca and almost up against her back. Waves of desire swelled within her. Grateful that he had taken the lead, she realized that, nonetheless, she had to make it clear that she chose him.

Ushca stepped back enough to press up against Straf'Tor, and at the same time, she reached around and took his hand, wrapping his arm around her waist. She felt him respond to her and knew the deal was sealed. He pulled her harder against him, leaned down, and pressed his face to her neck.

"I choose you, Straf'Tor," she whispered into his ear.

His hot breath brushed over her. "Finally," was all he said.

Straf'Tor and Ushca were lost in their own world. Most of the inhabitants of Kthama had been aware for some time that the two desired each other. Seeing it come together before their eyes was an unexpected pleasure.

E'ranale and Moc'Tor also sat watching as, finally, the long-denied yearning between Straf'Tor and Ushca came to a head. When the couple suddenly realized they were still in the common area with all eyes upon them, Ushca took Straf'Tor's hand and led him out of the room.

Also watching was Toniss. Freed from Straf'Tor, she made a beeline for the other side of the room, where Trak had been standing quietly, staring a hole into her.

E'ranale and Moc'Tor looked at each other.

"I did not see that coming," said Moc'Tor. "But I should have known after Trak attacked Straf when Toniss's name came up. Wait; you told me Toniss is seeded. Will that not complicate things with her and Trak?"

"You are assuming the offling she carries was seeded by Straf," E'ranale answered with a chuckle.

"Trak?" asked Moc'Tor. "That explains everything."

Now everyone was watching Toniss and Trak

circle each other like creatures in heat. The sexual tension filled the room.

"Well, this ought to get things going for the others!" exclaimed E'ranale.

"No doubt," Moc'Tor laughed. "And I am glad for them." With fire in his own eyes, he pretended to leer at E'ranale.

Over the next few weeks, many of the females chose males to mate with. There were a few skirmishes, but the pairing up went surprisingly well, proving what E'ranale had predicted; most of them did have preferences. For whatever reason, some of the females did not choose—in some cases because the contagion had left significantly fewer males than females.

Most of the sickness had left, and the husks of all who had died had been returned to the Great Spirit by ritual fire. However, despite the seeming calm, Moc'Tor was not relaxed. For one thing, Norcab, in particular, had been absent from the common areas.

First Guard Dochrohan found the Guardian walking outside Kthama. "Moc'Tor!" he called out.

The Leader stopped and waited.

"There is something you need to know. Norcab

has been meeting in secret with several of the younger males."

"I am aware of it," he said, resuming his walk with Dochrohan beside him.

"Are you also aware of the topic of the meetings?"

"I would imagine my removal from leadership, with or without my demise."

"Yes, though I am not sure which they have decided upon."

"I will deal with it at the appropriate time, Dochrohan, though I do appreciate the information."

"There are quite a few of them, Moc'Tor— although I am not questioning your strength or fighting ability."

"Did you ever have to fight a Sarius snake, Dochrohan?"

"No, I cannot say that I have. But I know they are treacherous and can grow up to three arm-lengths and as thick as a grown male's thigh."

"Yes. And if you let yourself be distracted by its size, you will fail. There is only one guaranteed way to dispatch it."

"And what is that?"

"Cut off the head. Without the head, no matter how big it is, the rest of the snake is no longer a threat." Moc'Tor stopped walking and turned to face the first guard. "However," he added, "I am not so blind that I do not know I may need help in this matter. I will appreciate any other information you discover. Males like Norcab are not males of honor."

"The other males and I will stand with you. Nysas has joined the group and will keep me informed of their plans."

"I am the only target, correct?"

"As far as I know." Dochrohan stared at Moc'Tor for a moment. "You are not suggesting—"

"That in his hatred of me Norcab might hurt E'ranale and our offling? I would not put it past him or any other male stupid enough to challenge a Guardian."

"Who would go so low as to hurt a female, let alone one with offling? I am tempted to fight you for the chance to kill him myself," said the first guard.

"Place your strongest male to watch discreetly over E'ranale and our offling—with instructions to kill Norcab on sight if he or anyone else in his group goes near them. However, unless he makes such a move and is dealt with beforehand, he is mine."

Norcab and his males were waiting for Moc'Tor in the mouth of a tunnel that opened onto the Great Chamber. Norcab had enlisted a group of about twenty to his cause of unseating the Leader. They were mostly younger males blinded by their drives, and with nothing to lose, had been enticed by Norcab. He had promised to strip the females of the power Moc'Tor had given them and grant the males the right to take at will any they wished to, even if the females refused to cooperate.

Moc'Tor's seventh sense had already alerted him to their presence. That and the heavy breathing that came from the passage.

As Moc'Tor neared the opening, Norcab stepped out of the shadows, blocking his path.

"You are in my way, Norcab."

"That is ironic. Because you are in my way, Moc'Tor."

"You are a fool. And I have no time for fools." Moc'Tor pushed Norcab out of his way but swung around and grabbed him by the back of the neck, catching him off guard. The Guardian easily swung him hard onto the rock floor, and Norcab's grab for Moc'Tor's ankles was met with a kick to the face. Blood spurted everywhere as Norcab's nose split with a resounding crack.

Enraged by the pain, he pulled himself onto all fours and lunged at Moc'Tor. Both bodies crashed to the floor, and the two giants rolled, each trying to gain the advantage. Norcab ended up on top with his hands around Moc'Tor's throat, but Moc'Tor brought up both his knees and pushed against his opponent's chest, catapulting Norcab several yards away. While Norcab was trying to get to his feet, Moc'Tor launched onto him and wrapped an arm around the rebel's neck, pulling hard to cut off his breath. Norcab clawed at Moc'Tor's arm, trying to get air.

Realizing that Norcab was losing, his band emerged from the shadows. Moc'Tor ignored them; his battle was first and foremost with Norcab, and without their Leader, they would most likely not be brave enough to pick up the fight.

By now, other Mothoc had entered the Great Chamber to watch the brutal battle taking place between the two behemoths. One of them ran to find Dochrohan, who had already heard and was on his way.

Moc'Tor knew that Norcab had only seconds left before passing out; it would be easy enough to crush his opponent's windpipe right then and there, but the Leader needed more than simply to kill him. He had to publicly destroy Norcab and any legacy of his defiance.

Seeing that the room was filling even further, Moc'Tor did not have to stall any longer. He released Norcab and moved away from him. "Get up. Get up and die like a warrior instead of the coward you are!"

Norcab gasped for breath in between coughing and spitting out the blood from his broken nose. He wiped his face and forced himself to his feet.

"Va! It is you who will die, Moc'Tor."

The Leader shook his head. "A coward and a fool both. Today is my lucky day."

At that moment, Dochrohan entered the room with his guards and made quick work of getting Norcab's band under control, ensuring that this would be a fair fight.

Arms out, the combatants circled each other and Moc'Tor moved closer to the rock wall behind him, trusting that his opponent would fall for the appearance of opportunity it presented. Norcab moved unsteadily, his gaze locked on Moc'Tor.

Suddenly, the Guardian dropped his guard and looked to the side as if distracted by something. Norcab lunged at him, and Moc'Tor timed it perfectly, sidestepping to let the hulking giant's momentum carry him head-first into the hard wall. Crumpled in a heap, Norcab clutched his head and moaned.

By now, the Great Chamber was filled with spectators.

Moc'Tor was spattered with fresh blood that formed a stark contrast to his thick silver hair. "Give it up, Norcab. Admit you are beaten. You are done."

"If you are so sure you have won, Moc'Tor, then kill me and get it over with."

"You are no match for me, Norcab," taunted Moc'Tor. "I will not kill an unworthy opponent, even one who rightfully deserves it."

Norcab raised his head and growled. His eyes were already swelling shut, and his hair was caked with the blood from his broken nose. "I will not stop until I have killed you and restored order to our people."

"You would not restore order. You would return our people to the path of destruction from which I delivered us all. And as for killing me, you are a greater imbecile than I realized. Cut your losses and get on with your life. There is nothing here for you but defeat, today and any other day on which you foolishly decide to challenge the Guardian."

Everyone was frozen in place. Norcab caught movement as E'ranale pressed her way through the crowd to stand in front of the other bystanders. Her hand flew to her face as she saw Moc'Tor and Norcab squared off in battle.

Norcab locked his gaze on E'ranale. Moc'Tor's blood ran cold.

"If I cannot kill you, Moc'Tor, I can at least make you wish I had." Norcab launched himself at E'ranale, who was standing exposed and defenseless only a few strides away.

The chamber seemed to split in two with the sound of Moc'Tor's rage as he flew after Norcab, felling him just inches from grasping E'ranale. As Moc'Tor brought Norcab to the floor, the first guard stepped in front of E'ranale, spear at the ready.

Driven by blind rage, Moc'Tor dragged Norcab to his feet, and holding him with both hands while bringing up one knee, slammed it into Norcab's head. Then he forced Norcab further down, and in one swift twist, snapped his neck before allowing the limp body to fall to the floor. The Guardian looked down at his own body, now drenched with his opponent's blood. Still enraged, panting, he stepped over Norcab's crumpled frame and faced the remainder of the rebel group.

"Anyone else?" he roared. "Anyone else want to threaten me—or my family? If you do, step up now. Do you think you are male enough to challenge me? Then speak up!"

Every member of Norcab's group looked terrified. Dochrohan's guards still had them lined up and chastened by spears poised for action.

Moc'Tor passed down the row, looking each in the eye. Most could not meet his gaze; they were no match for the Guardian, not at any level. "Va! I thought not." Moc'Tor spat at their feet. "Take a good look at your champion. From now on, each of you is forbidden to be in the same room as E'ranale. Dochrohan, if any one of them is, you or your guards are to kill him on sight."

"We have done nothing, Moc'Tor!"

Moc'Tor turned and walked over to stand directly in front of the speaker. He was saddened to see it was Warnak, one whom he had thought had some promise.

"Nothing? Conspiring against your Leader is nothing? You have not done nothing. But I will grant you one point, Warnak; you are nothing because anyone who stands with a coward who would attack a female is nothing. And I will not spend one moment having my family looking over their shoulders at nothing."

In the swiftest of motions, Moc'Tor seized the spear from the guard who stood behind Warnak, raised it overhead, and drove it straight down into

Warnak's center, piercing the chest cavity. Killed instantly, Warnak remained upright, suspended by the spear. Moc'Tor rose, repositioned his grip higher on the shaft, and forced the spear down until it exited between Warnak's legs. He then stepped back and let the impaled body fall as he had Norcab's. A river of red gushed from the still twitching form.

For a moment, Moc'Tor stood watching before stepping over the carnage. "Remove this garbage," he ordered Dochrohan.

Then he turned back to face the rest of the rebellious band. "Because of Warnak's foolishness, the severity of your punishment has just been increased. Dochrohan, have your guards give them a few moments to collect their Keeping Stones, then escort them out of Kthama."

Turning to the rebels, Moc'Tor growled, "I do not know what awaits you out there, but you can see what waits for you here should you be stupid enough to return." He glanced first at Norcab's lifeless husk and then at Warnak's. "Dochrohan, you and your guards listen carefully. If any of them returns, kill him on sight and hang his body near the entrance to rot, a reminder for the rest of you who think they can defy me or threaten my family."

Choking down tears, E'ranale turned away from the gore. She knew Warnak's mother well, and her heart broke for the female who would soon learn that her oldest offling had paid the ultimate price for his poor choice in alliances. She knew that Moc'Tor had done what must be done, but it sickened her that it had come to this. She wanted to run from the room but steeled herself to wait for Moc'Tor as anything less would be seen as a lack of support for his actions.

Her mate came over to her, pressed his hand against the small of her back, and guided her from the room.

"Be strong," he said as they continued on to their quarters. "You are staying with me tonight. And every night for the foreseeable future."

Once alone, E'ranale broke down. Moc'Tor wanted to pull her to him, but he was still covered in blood.

"Lie down and relax. I will be back once I have cleaned up."

Moc'Tor stepped into the private area before realizing exactly how bloody he was. Though reluctant to leave her, he went to clean himself up in the males' bathing area.

"No good choices," he muttered as he dipped into the water, hating it and knowing it would take hours for him to dry. When he was finished, he squeezed as much of the water as possible from his coat.

He returned damp but clean to find E'ranale curled up on her side, fast asleep. For once, he regretted his prohibition against fire inside Kthama. He longed to sit outside to dry next to one of Drit's raging, evening fires but could not leave E'ranale alone. He stretched out alongside her, hoping she would somehow feel his presence.

Sometime in the middle of the night, E'ranale sat up with a start, twisting wildly about as if fighting someone. Moc'Tor sat up immediately and gently grabbed her flailing arms.

"E'ranale, wake up. Wake up; I am right here. It is only a dream."

E'ranale looked at Moc'Tor hazily, then flung her arms around his damp neck and sobbed. He held her tight against him as her tears released some of the horrors she had witnessed earlier.

"I know E'ranale, it was terrible, but you know there was no other way."

E'ranale's tears leaked more wetness into Moc'-Tor's heavy silver coat. She squeezed her eyes closed and clung to him tighter, trying to shut out the images of the crumpled and mangled bodies lying on the rock floor. "I have never seen such blood and gore. And I cannot stop thinking of Warnak's mother. Every time she passes down the corridor— We will never get the stain out, Moc'Tor."

"E'ranale, I do not want the stain out. It must stay as a reminder to others who may think to challenge my authority."

"What will happen to them?"

"Those I banished? They will live a life of struggle and hardship unless they find another community to take them in. But that is doubtful. Few

Leaders would take on young males in the prime of their drives who have been ejected from their own people. Banishment is one of the worst punishments we can impose. If they are wise, they will try to return."

"But I thought you said that if they return, they are to be killed on sight?"

"Yes. Exactly. A quick death would be better than the slow, agonizing death awaiting them in banishment."

CHAPTER 6

All eyes in the room were still on Haan. They waited for him to continue his story, yet he remained silent as if considering whether to continue.

"Haan, you said that your laws forbade contact between us. Yet you made contact," stated Kurak'Kahn.

Haan continued his story, adding his rough Handspeak to help make himself clearer. "Hakani, my mate, and my son Akar'Tor were both sick. They needed help from the Akassa Healer, Adia. Without Adia's help, my family would have died. Yes, contact is forbidden, but I accepted the risk. Now that contact has been made, the damage has been done. I must now meet with you in hopes of forming strong ties between all our people."

The more the Sarnonn spoke, the more easily they could understand him.

"We welcome your contact, Haan. We greet you with open arms," said Kurak'Kahn.

"Your Healer, Adia, saved my mate, Hakani. I know there was past trouble between Khon'Tor and Hakani. I now know that Hakani lied to me about much of what went on between her and Khon'Tor. There will be no trouble between us. Except perhaps over Akar'Tor."

Khon'Tor sighed; he had been hoping that the subject would not come up. He had no intention of accepting Akar'Tor—let alone welcoming him—into the community. The interest in Tehya was reason enough to bar him, but Akar'Tor's behavior that morning had only strengthened Khon'Tor's determination to refuse his presence at Kthama. And he did not want the High Council interfering as they had in the past. Unless it was to lift the restriction that only a blood relative might inherit the leadership—which he highly doubted—Khon'Tor wanted no remarks about this situation from the High Council.

Then as if on cue, Kurak'Kahn asked, "What are your plans for Akar'Tor, Khon'Tor?"

Rok, thought Khon'Tor. "I would prefer not to discuss it in this forum, Overseer. I believe we have more pressing matters at hand."

"Very well," said Kurak'Kahn. But Khon'Tor could read in his eyes that the Overseer was not going to let the matter drop.

Adia turned to Haan. "Do you wish to continue?"

"I need to send word to Hakani that Akar is here. When I left, we were not certain where he had gone."

So that was what was on his mind. Yes, better he gets word to her than we have Hakani show up here looking for them both, thought Khon'Tor. "Perhaps a short recess, Overseer?" he asked.

"Very well. We can reconvene a little later. Anyone wishing to stay and discuss what we have learned so far, please do so. Otherwise, we will see you all after mid-meal."

Acaraho moved away from his seat next to Adia and, now in his position of High Protector, stepped to the door.

"I will meet you in the Great Chamber," Adia said to him as she brushed past. After everyone had filtered out, except those staying back to speak with Kurak'Kahn, Acaraho also turned to leave.

"Commander," said Kurak'Kahn.

Acaraho turned to face him. "Yes, Overseer?"

"I do not know what to make of this. Do you have an opinion you wish to share with me?"

"About what in particular?"

"About Haan's presence here. Why now? I understand that he seeded Hakani and that they needed the help of your Healer—Adia—but this has gone beyond that. There is no reason for him to be here now that Hakani and Akar'Tor are well—is there?"

"I understand your question. However, I do believe that Haan also wants something from us. I imagine help in some further way. In return, he is willing to share information. Hopefully, it is a fair exchange. I would feel more comfortable, though, if he would state his request upfront."

"Perhaps it will become more obvious as the story unfolds. You believe that he is going to tell us more?"

"We will have to wait and see. We cannot rush the process and risk losing this opportunity. It may never come again."

Kurak'Kahn nodded, and Acaraho took his leave.

Haan stopped by Akar'Tor's solitary lodgings on his way out. "I am going to send a message to your mother that you came here as she suspected. Are you ready to go home now?"

Akar'Tor frowned, "No. I am not going back. I am going to stay here and demand that Khon'Tor teach me what I need to know so I can be the next Leader."

Haan shook his head. "You have destroyed your chances here, Akar. I can see it clearly in Khon'Tor. Nothing you do will change his mind. I am sorry to be so harsh with you, but you need to grow up and face the facts. What you did this morning was inexcusable. You need to return to Kayerm, take your place among our people, and put Kthama from your mind."

Akar'Tor glared at his father. *Now my own father is no longer on my side. Khon'Tor has turned everyone against me. Father is wrong, I will make him accept me, or I will make him pay for it. Khon'Tor is no better than I am. We are practically the same person only I am younger than him. He has no right to have a young mate like Tehya. She should be mine and not his. The idea of him mating her is disgusting!*

Haan could see that Akar'Tor had shut out everything he had just said. "You are headed for a hard lesson, son. I am sorry I cannot spare you from it, but apparently, it is what you need in order to learn what it is to become a real male—and someone worthy of being followed."

With that, Haan left and went to find one of his people, Yar, concealed outside Kthama, to send a message back to Hakani.

❍

Hakani sat nursing Kalli when Yar brought word that Akar'Tor had indeed gone to Kthama. And now Haan was also there. How she wished she was at Kthama too, yet she was luckier than most females as she had the help of Haan's aides and her friends, Haaka and Sastak. When Kalli finished, Hakani lay back and curled around her daughter, thinking about Akar'Tor.

I do not wonder why he went back. But I wonder how long before he finds out he will never fit in? He has none of the teachings of our culture. He hunts like a Sassen. He thinks like a Sassen. He does not know how to live within such a structured community as Kthama. He is short-tempered like both Khon'Tor and me, and will not deal well with the restrictions that would be necessary for him to live among them. Worst of all, Khon'Tor will never accept him. No doubt, his young Tehya will produce offspring before too long.

But then, if Khon'Tor were out of the way, could I not return to Kthama? If Akar'Tor could be the Leader of the People, that would put me back into a position of influence, if not authority. And what of that little one? I doubt there is any fire in her. —Has he tired of bedding her yet? Have his tastes for domination stirred?

So, there is still hope. Once she finds out what he is truly like, she will not have the strength to bear it and will leave him. And that might be the time to strike— when he is at his weakest. If Akar and I work together, perhaps he can position himself in a place of leadership at Kthama, after which it will be possible for me to return as his mother and therefore as a person of great influence."

Urilla Wuti, Adia, and Acaraho sat together in the Great Chamber to eat. With everything that was going on, Acaraho and Adia spent little time in their quarters except to sleep and recharge.

"Urilla Wuti, what do you think of Haan's story?" asked Adia.

"He is more intelligent than he comes across as— that was an important point you made to the High Council, Adia."

"Yes. You remember, when it came time to induce Hakani's unborn offspring early, I had to make him understand that we had to take the chance. That though they could still die, there was no possibility that either would survive if the offspring were born naturally. I was so afraid he would go on a rampage if I failed and lost the offspring. He had already had an earlier confrontation with Khon'Tor. In a battle between our two tribes, our people would not stand a chance. So I made that Connection with him. I tried to keep it tight and shallow, as you taught me. But, remember, I could not control the stream of the Connection, Urilla Wuti. His consciousness was so strong. It was like being sucked underwater. If it had not been for your intercession, I could never have disconnected, and I do not know what would have happened after that."

"I felt that they still existed, but I did not know they were so close. I believe they have a way to cloak their existence," said Urilla Wuti.

Acaraho's attention perked up. "They are masters at hiding. It might be in the nature of their hair covering; it has a kind of shimmering quality that blends with the surroundings. But perhaps there is more to it, as you are suggesting, Urilla Wuti.

"We know— No, let me start over because we are finding that what we thought we knew is not necessarily true. We *believed* that in the past, the males, as well as the females, held the seventh sense. Perhaps it was retained in the Sarnonn, whereas it was bred out of us. It is clear we carry more of the Brothers' blood in us than they do."

"Khon'Tor should be here for this discussion," said Acaraho, thoughtfully, just as Khon'Tor and Tehya rounded the corner.

He waved them over. "We were discussing Haan."

Khon'Tor chuckled. "As I am sure everyone else on the High Council is doing."

Acaraho recapped their discussion about the possibility of Haan's having mental powers they did not possess.

When he had finished, Khon'Tor said, "The Mothoc had much longer lifespans. I imagine that was also bred out of us; we live over twice as long as the Brothers, but we live nowhere near the Mothoc's apparent longevity. Haan said his parent's parents were here at Kthama."

"The story is fascinating," said Acaraho, "but when we reconvene, perhaps we should focus on another area for a few moments. I want to know what Haan wants from us. And why his people seem to be afraid of us."

Both the females looked at Acaraho with raised eyebrows.

"Earlier, when Haan's sentry came to tell us he

got our message, he seemed very nervous. Awan also noticed it. There was no way we misinterpreted it—he was afraid. As were the five in the valley, whom I met when Haan showed me the tree breaks."

"Perhaps it is not us, exactly," said Khon'Tor. "Maybe it is something *about us* instead. They are certainly not afraid to take us on physically—or at least Haan has proven he is not."

"And what about Akar'Tor—" Acaraho looked across at Khon'Tor.

"He cannot stay. I will not allow it."

"It may not be your choice—"

"That has occurred to me, too. His timing could not have been worse for me. Staging that in front of the High Council. Was he smart enough to think of that himself? Or was someone else behind it?" said Khon'Tor, clearly meaning Hakani.

"The High Council should not intervene, Khon'-Tor," said Urilla Wuti.

"What we think they should or should not do seems not to influence what they decide to do. In the past, they have proven that their lines are blurred when it comes to my jurisdiction over my own people. And with the seriousness of the situation, they seem prone to bending the rules. Adia and Acaraho, you are examples of that, though I am glad that at last you were officially allowed to be paired."

Adia noticed that Tehya was staring off into nothingness. Intercepting the glance, Khon'Tor also saw it.

"What is wrong, Tehya?" he asked.

Tehya hung her head. "If I had not lost your offspring, then Akar'Tor's claim would not have the power it does, being your only living offspring."

Everyone at the table suddenly realized that Tehya was the only one who did not know that Nootau and Nimida were also Khon'Tor's offspring. But it was Khon'Tor's place to reveal that truth, despite the fact that it kept Tehya in the dark.

Secrets, thought Knon'Tor. *I once thought them to be a strength. Now I see them only to be weaknesses. And Hakani holds a powerful one—she knows that Nootau is Adia's by my seed. At some point, I may have to confess my crime to Tehya.*

"Surely they can see that Akar'Tor has no grounds other than his claim of the bloodline. And his association with Hakani makes it all too volatile," added Adia.

"Khon'Tor," she continued, "We will support you in resisting their interference. The issues between you and Akar'Tor need to remain just that—between you and him. The High Council members should understand what it would mean to have Hakani's influence back among us. She has done damage enough for a Sarnonn's lifetime, let alone one of ours."

"For what it is worth, Haan made it clear to his son that he was out of line this morning." Khon'Tor swung his leg over the rock bench he had straddled,

"It is time we should be getting back." He got up, and Tehya and the others followed his lead.

As they left the eating area, they met Akar'Tor coming their way escorted by the two guards assigned to watch him. Khon'Tor immediately stepped around in front and protectively sandwiched Tehya behind him and in front of Acaraho.

"Good afternoon, *Father*," Akar'Tor sneered. "I hope you do not mind if I leave my captivity in order to eat?"

"The obvious truth is that you are not a captive, Akar. If you were, you would not be standing here in front of me now."

Akar'Tor peered around Khon'Tor, trying to see Tehya.

Khon'Tor leaned to the side, blocking his line of sight. "What is it you want?"

"I told you. I need something to eat."

"What do you want here, Akar? Are you so misguided that you honestly think you have a place here at Kthama?"

"The law says I do, as your son," Akar'Tor spat out in reply.

That he could switch from so insolent one moment to so angry the next, surprised Khon'Tor.

"The fact that my blood may or may not run in your veins is not an entitlement to leadership. It is only a result of ill-advised choices on my part."

"May or *may not* run in my veins? You question that you seeded me? By the Great Spirit, look at me!"

Khon'Tor scoffed. "Your mother was not the most faithful of mates, Akar. Or did she not tell you that side of the story?"

Acaraho and Adia looked at each other. What Khon'Tor was suggesting was ludicrous; Akar'Tor was an exact duplicate of him.

Akar'Tor raised his arm as if to strike Khon'Tor, who immediately grabbed it below the wrist and held it in an iron grip. Khon'Tor then increased the pressure and twisted, forcing Akar'Tor down to the ground on his knees in front of him. "Do not even think of it, Akar. You are not welcome here. And you cannot force your way into a position that you have not earned. I do not care on what you base your claim."

"You are one to talk about mating practices, Khon'Tor. Does your young mate—" He let out a cry as Khon'Tor twisted his arm further, stopping him mid-sentence, and nearly breaking it at the elbow. Then he bent over and placed his other hand on Akar'Tor's shoulder, pressing him deeper into the hard floor.

"Another twist, Akar, and I will relieve you of the use of your arm forever. Choose wisely. Life as a smart-mouthed cripple or your first lesson in exercising discretion? Which is it to be?"

Tehya looked horrified. She instinctively stepped back until the wall of Acaraho's chest halted her.

"I concede," Akar'Tor gasped out.

Khon'Tor did not release him immediately. He

stooped over until he was level to Akar'Tor's ear. "Breathe one more word *ever* about what you think went on here before," Khon'Tor whispered, "and I will end you before you can take a second breath. And I promise you, while you will not enjoy it, I certainly will. Just as I enjoyed every *twisted* thing I did to your mother."

The Leader released Akar'Tor and straightened up, throwing a heart-stopping glance at the Healer in case she had any thought of tending to him.

Akar'Tor slumped to the ground, grasping his bruised arm with his other hand.

Khon'Tor turned, took Tehya's hand, and led her around the crumpled form still incapacitated on the rock floor in front of them.

"Enjoy your meal, Akar. Then *go home*," he said as he walked away without a backward glance.

The two guards flanked Akar'Tor, waiting for him to recover but making no attempt to help him to his feet; they had seen the searing look the Leader had given Adia.

Almost all the Leaders were back in the meeting room in response to the special sounding of the Call To Assembly Horn, as ordered by Acaraho. Khon'Tor stood against a rock wall, deep in reflection.

I lost control. I should never have said those things to Akar. If from whatever his mother told him, he believed he had reason to hate me, I just confirmed it. I think I have changed, but have I? How easily I turned back to savagery. And I enjoyed it. He is my own son, my own blood, yet I would welcome the chance to beat him into submission, or worse. Is it because he is so closely tied to Hakani? Or is it because he threatens Tehya? Where is the line between righteous anger and bloodlust? I do not know. I do not know. The truth is, despite the consequences and whatever the reason, part of me is just waiting for justification, an excuse, to kill him.

Khon'Tor's head hung lost in thought but snapped up when he felt Tehya's soft hand on his arm. He turned to see her beautiful eyes looking up into his.

"It is time to begin. The Overseer has just entered. And so has Haan."

He turned and went to sit down with her, cherishing the feel of her tiny hand enveloped in his.

☾

Kurak'Kahn stood and addressed the group. "Before we continue, does anyone have anything they wish to say?"

Risik'Tar, Leader of the Great Pines, rose. "Those of us who spoke together during the meal have an almost endless list of questions, but we think it is best that Haan continues with what he came to share. Most likely, many questions will be answered as he continues his story."

Turning to Haan, the Overseer asked, "Haan, is there more you wish to tell?"

Haan had slid down and sat against the rock wall as was now his custom. Those in attendance once again involuntarily gasped as he stood and continued his story. "The times of unrest continued among the Mothoc. Those who could not accept the females owning the power to choose left Kthama. Some joined other communities, others left and were not heard of again, perhaps having perished. The population shrank. Offling became fewer and fewer. Those who did survive were sometimes addled or sick. The Great Spirit's condemnation continued. Ideas of change were still met with harsh resistance. But change eventually came."

CHAPTER 7

M oc'Tor's son, Dak'Tor, threw his first spear, impaling the target perfectly. The Guardian retrieved the weapon and handed it back to him.

"Again."

"I am tired, Father."

"It does not matter. Set your physical body aside. A warrior who nurses his weaknesses will never build his strengths. Now, again."

E'ranale and Oragur approached the two. Without turning, Moc'Tor guessed the content of the message they were bringing.

"Another deadborn?"

It was Oragur who spoke. "Yes. Unfortunately."

"There are now more born dead than alive, and some of those who live seem to be sick or unstable. Starting with Trestle," sighed the Leader.

"Trestle is nearly full-grown, and his mind is still that of an offling," agreed E'ranale.

Moc'Tor closed his eyes and gave thanks for the health of his own offling and said a prayer for E'ranale's belly, once again swollen. So many others were not as fortunate.

"The females are saying the male's seed is ruined, poisoned. They are heartbroken and angry," said Oragur.

Moc'Tor stopped and took the spear from his son's hand. Placing his other hand on Dak'Tor's head, he said, "Alright, that is enough for today. Go and find your sisters and cousins."

He watched the offling scamper off. "Something has to change. We have to change."

"What are you thinking, Moc'Tor?" asked E'ranale.

As he spoke, Moc'Tor put his hand on her belly, and she placed her hands over his, resting them there. "It is time for the Leaders and what is left of the other communities to come together. We cannot solve this problem in isolation. Perhaps, if we combine our efforts, we can come up with a solution. We cannot stand by and let our people pass from Etera."

Moc'Tor sent messengers up and down the Mother Stream and into the far reaches of the outer regions.

The words were simple, "Leaders and Healers, come to Kthama at the next full moon. We must join together, or all will be lost."

As the time passed, he readied Kthama for what he hoped would be a large assembly. Somehow, the excitement of something different breathed new life into his community. He knew they needed hope. If he could give them nothing else, he could at least give them that.

❂

As the full moon broke through the clouds over Kthama, the turnout for the first Leader's meeting was a resounding success; the cave system was once again pressed to overflowing.

Enjoying a brief moment of solitude, Moc'Tor stood with his face to the moonlight and asked the Great Spirit for guidance and wisdom. The next morning between the first meal and the midday meal, he would address the other Leaders and their Healers.

❂

As he had a hundred times before, Moc'Tor headed for the front of the room, head held high, with the Leader's Staff in his hand. This time, however, many different eyes followed his massive silver-coated frame as he passed by. To his right stood Oragur and

Drit, to his left, E'ranale, his First Choice. He signaled for them to be seated and turned to address the large group of Leaders and Healers.

"Thank you for coming to Kthama. This is a momentous occasion, and we honor your presence with us—the first time we, as Leaders, have come together in unity. I hope you will find value in our assembly and that we will continue these meetings past our current crisis.

"I know that many of you will still be tired after a long journey here, and for that reason, some of our females will be bringing refreshments so you may relax somewhat before we move to a private meeting room to conduct our business."

A while later, in the large, secluded room, Moc'Tor got down to the issues before them.

"Ever since the sickness reduced our numbers, we have struggled with repopulation. Despite all our efforts, we seem to have come to an impasse. When our females do become seeded, many of the offling die or are born impaired. I know it is the same for your people. Each of you is in a position of influence. Each of you has a community that looks to you for guidance and protection. As for me, I feel that for a long time, I have failed in both regards. The mantle of leadership can become heavy at times. Perhaps, together as one people, we can solve our problems."

Solok'Tar from the Great Pines stood to speak. "As Leader, I have willingly borne alone the burden of my people. But I believe Moc'Tor is right. It is time now that we band together and bring our collective wisdom to bear on this problem. If we do not, we will eventually all perish. Let us not forget our duty to Etera."

Next rose Hatos'Mok of the Deep Valley.

"We have done as you did, Moc'Tor. We gave our females the right to choose with whom to mate. At first, there was much dissent among the males. Uprisings. But that is behind us, and it was the right decision. But still, we have no favor with the Great Spirit. And the females' heartache at holding their deadborn is turning to anger. They demand solutions. They demand their right to produce life, and they look to me for answers. Yet I have none to give. I, too, welcome this new community of leadership."

Oragur stood to speak, "Not all the male seed is sour. Some males in each community are fathering live, healthy offling."

Moc'Tor took back the floor. "Oragur is right; some of our offling are still being born healthy, so all is not lost, but we need to maximize the benefit. Perhaps it is time for another change. When our numbers were overflowing, we had enough healthy young adults for matings within our own communities. Now, perhaps it is time to consider an exchange."

Those present started talking among themselves.

"An exchange? What kind of exchange?" The anonymous question came from the middle of the crowd.

"An exchange of females. Or of males. Instead of mating within our own communities, as they come of age, our young adults could be paired with suitable mates from another community."

"And make them leave their homes to live with strangers?" It was a different voice this time.

"You make it sound like exile," the Guardian continued. "They would be welcomed to their new community, would they not? The promise of healthy new offling? New bloodlines? It should be a cause for celebration. In time it could become voluntary—but not until we have fully re-established our numbers."

"It would be unpopular, Moc'Tor!"

He laughed. "I have come up with unpopular decisions before, Krasus'Nol. It is one of my gifts. Yes, it will be unpopular, but only for the first generation or so. The next generations raised in this way will expect it, accept it as part of our culture. And further, it will knit us closer together. We have been isolated from each other for far too long. In each of our communities, the numbers are low; we have half-siblings and cousins mating with each other. Perhaps that is also part of our losing favor with the Great Spirit. Perhaps that is part of the reason why those of our offling who survive are born unhealthy."

Another voice arose, "We cannot change this quickly, Moc'Tor. What you ask is impossible."

"If what I ask is impossible, then we are all doomed. Within a few generations, the Mothoc will no longer walk the land. What will happen when we are not here to worship Etera and protect her? Who will serve as keepers of the forest? What eyes will look out at the beauty of this world and give thanks and honor her bounty? Who will look after and protect the Others as we have always done? Our homes will stand, and the Mother Stream will flow, but without the Mothoc. And without us, the flow of the creative breath of the Great Spirit, which sustains our world, the flow of the Aezaitera, will weaken. Without the Mothoc and the Guardian, the future of Etera is at risk."

Moc'Tor walked closer to the group. "Dealing with change has always been our greatest challenge. We have to be backed against a wall with one last breath remaining before we will even consider it. But we cannot wait for that now. If we wait until change is comfortable, change will never come. If we wait until we want to change, the opportunity will have passed. It will be too late. If we must wait until change is forced upon us to open our minds to it, well, that time is here.

"So, instead of resisting change, I am asking you to embrace it. I am challenging you to embrace it. If I may be so bold, I am telling you that as a Leader, it is your responsibility to your people to require it. Order it. Shove it down their throats if you have to. Bear their wrath. Do whatever it takes but be the Leader.

Be strong enough to do whatever is necessary to ensure that our people do not disappear from Etera. Without us, Etera's lifeblood will weaken and dry up, and eventually, all life upon her will pass into history."

As his speech ended, a commotion in the back of the room diverted everyone's attention. Two large Mothoc guards entered the room dragging a young male and followed closely by an older female. The guards looked around, realizing they had disturbed the meeting but unsure what else they could have done.

Moc'Tor strode toward them. "What is it? What is the problem?" He recognized Trestle suspended between the guards—the mentally impaired male he had been speaking about not long ago.

"It is Trestle, Moc'Tor. We found him near the Others' territory. He has been missing for days, and after finding no sign of him on our own land, our search finally widened to the land that borders their territory."

Moc'Tor looked at Trestle, who seemed terrified.

"Moc'Tor, he was with one of the Others."

Moc'Tor turned his eyes from Trestle to the guards.

"And?" The Guardian's eyes were steely cold.

"A maiden, Moc'Tor. He was about to take her without her consent. Or at least try to."

Moc'Tor closed his eyes as Trestle's mother rushed over and grabbed her son's arm. She quickly let go when the Leader opened his eyes and looked down at her. "Please, Moc'Tor," she begged. "We have been searching for him. He does not know any better. None of our females will have him. He does not understand; he has seen others of our people similarly occupied. He did not mean any harm."

Moc'Tor hated that this was the mother of Warnak, the defiant young male he had impaled years ago over Norcab's revolt. Now, once again, more heartache for this poor female who has done nothing to deserve any of it. "Where is the maiden?"

"We pulled him off her. She had passed out, no doubt from fear."

"Are you sure he did not—"

"No, Guardian, we caught him in time. If he had, no doubt it would have killed her. She could never have accepted the size of him. He would have torn her open beyond survival if she had not first died of fright."

"Clean him up, feed him, and confine him. I will deal with this later."

The accused's mother looked up at him pleadingly before following the guards as they led Trestle away.

"Leaders and Healers," Moc'Tor resumed. "Let us take a short break as it is almost time for the evening meal that our females have laid out for you in the Great Chamber. Discuss these problems among yourselves and bring back your thoughts when we meet here afterward."

Outside the meeting room, E'ranale approached Moc'Tor. "Trestle. What happened?"

"He almost violated one of the Others."

"Violated?"

"Without her consent."

"Moc'Tor, it would have killed her!"

"He almost mated her. They stopped him in time. We do not know that he harmed her other than nearly scaring her to death."

Oragur joined them. "This is a serious transgression, Moc'Tor. Perhaps it would be best to make her disappear."

Moc'Tor turned, grabbed Oragur by the throat, and pushed him back, pinning him to the wall. "Do not tell me how serious this is, Healer. I am well aware of the trouble Trestle has caused us all because of his mental impairment, but do not ever suggest doing anything of the sort to an innocent to cover up our sin. We are the Mothoc. The breath of Etera! Though they do not know it, we look after the Others. And above even that, you are a Healer; it is your job to foster life, not to take it. What is wrong with you? Va!"

He released Oragur, who rubbed his throat and glanced at E'ranale. She also looked as if she was about to snap.

"Enough! Enough." Moc'Tor threw up his arms. "Enough for now. I will be in my quarters."

"Are you not going after him?" Oragur asked E'ranale.

"Go after him? I am not going after him. But if you would like to, be my guest."

Oragur rubbed his neck some more. "No. I think it is better that he has some time to himself."

After a while, E'ranale did go to find Moc'Tor. He was lying on the arrangement of leaves and mosses covered by a hide that, together, made up their sleeping mat. It was unusual to find him stretched out there in the middle of the day.

"Moc'Tor?" she asked as she entered.

"You may join me if you wish. It is safe; I will not bite your head off as I did with Oragur. I have no more answers, E'ranale. The females are about to revolt. I am tired of the fires that constantly burn for our dead offling, and I can only imagine how the mothers feel. Now we have Trestle, who almost violated one of the Others' maidens. And a room full of Leaders and Healers expecting me to have a solution. Why did I think it was a good idea to bring everyone together?"

"Because it was a good idea. Not just a good idea; it was a great idea. The Leaders need a way to come together and share their counsel with each other, and because most of the Leaders and their Healers— if not all—are here at the same time, decisions can immediately be agreed upon. And your idea of exchanging the youth was inspired."

"Why are my inspired ideas always so unpopular?"

"It is as you said; you have a gift."

Moc'Tor gave her a sideways look and pulled her over to him. "Make me forget about it all for a while, E'ranale. Or are you too close to delivering?"

"I am, but some of the visiting females have taught me a few tricks for times such as this."

"Tricks?"

E'ranale chuckled.

"You will see. Just lie back and close your eyes. And no matter what happens, keep them closed. Then afterward, I have something related that I need to share with you, also learned from those females who are visiting us."

Moc'Tor stretched out and let out a huge sigh, waiting for her to straddle him. But within seconds of closing his eyes, they flew wide open. "E'ranale! What the—" He partially sat up and looked down at her.

"Sssh, relax. Trust me, Moc'Tor, you will find this enjoyable. And I promise I will not bite."

Moc'Tor did as she asked and received one of the biggest and most pleasurable surprises of his life.

The Guardian did not realize he had fallen asleep until he woke up. E'ranale lay beside him, still asleep. He sat up for a moment and then allowed himself to flop back down, enjoying the relief from stress that his mate had so generously provided him.

Unfortunately, he was robbed of the moment by someone arriving at the entrance to their quarters.

"Who is there?"

"Drit, Leader. They are re-assembling; I thought you would want to know."

"Thank you. I will be right there."

Moc'Tor reached over and roused his mate. She should be in attendance when the meeting reconvened.

She blinked and finally looked up at him.

"We need to go. We both fell asleep."

"Alright, I am coming."

"E'ranale."

"Yes?"

"Before we go, I do not know what to say. What you did to me—I thought I had experienced everything."

E'ranale smiled, pleased she had satisfied him.

"You are happy because I just proved your point, Guardian, that an exchange of ideas is a good thing!"

He laughed, and her eyes lit up at seeing the stress leave his face, even for a moment.

"Later, we will talk more about what you did."

E'ranale chuckled and rose to leave with her mate.

Moc'Tor could feel the agitation in the room as he entered. Groups of Leaders and Healers were standing grouped together in discussion. Others had taken a seat and were talking to their neighbors. Moc'Tor checked his senses again. No, not agitation. Excitement. Perhaps even a tinge of hope.

His confidence renewed, he called for their attention.

"Let us return and focus. Now that we have had a break, does anyone have anything to add?"

Solok'Tar stood to speak. "I cannot speak for the others, but I support your idea, Moc'Tor. However, I think we need a smaller circle to work out the details."

Moc'Tor looked at the faces staring back at him. Many of them showed approval, but many were blank. He could not tell how much overall support his idea had. "Take a position so we can see where we are. Everyone who supports the idea of exchanging mating-age young, please stand up."

The vast majority of those in the room stood. Moc'Tor suppressed a smile of relief.

"I agree with Solok'Tar of the Great Pines," Cha'Kahn said. "We need a smaller group to determine how to put this into motion. Who among us has a mind for detail? If we do this, we must keep records. We will have to find a way to mark down our decisions."

"You mean like the marks on the Keeping Stones?" queried Moc'Tor. Each individual was given a stone at birth, upon which was recorded the significant events of their life.

"Similar, but more detailed. So we know who has mated with whom from which family."

There was a nodding of heads, and several looked as if they would volunteer.

"It is a good idea. Anyone interested in working on it, meet me after we have finished this discussion. Now, are there any other questions or observations?"

"How do we quiet the females?"

Moc'Tor recognized Tarris'Kahn, son of Cha'Kahn, from the tiny community of Khire immediately up the Mother Stream. "They are demanding their right to reproduce. They are saying that the males caused the ire of the Great Spirit. That we were punished with the sickness that took so many of us and fouled our seed. But they do not believe they should be denied offling because of our sins."

"What exactly are they asking for?"

"An abomination, Guardian. They are asking for permission to commit an abomination."

"Great. That is great news, Tarris'Kahn," Moc'Tor replied.

"*Va*, Moc'Tor! You did not hear me! I said they are asking for us to participate in an abomination against the Great Spirit."

"I heard you perfectly, Tarris'Kahn. But what you are calling an abomination may be the solution we are looking for. Regardless of the merits of their idea, this may be just what we need. We must learn to think in new ways. Try new things, be open to what we would never accept before, or that would never occur to us if our backs were not against the wall. Perhaps even ideas that we consider an abomination, because at the root of them may be an inspired idea that will bring us to the perfect solution. Now, just what is this abomination the females are proposing?"

"They want to mate with the Others."

Moc'Tor blinked. He rubbed his chin and then crossed his arms over his chest. He looked at E'ranale, who raised her eyebrows and nodded at him.

"Excuse me," he said, holding up one finger as he stepped over to speak with his mate. "You knew about this and did not tell me?"

"I was going to."

"Then why did you not?"

"You fell asleep."

Moc'Tor cleared his throat. "Oh. Alright. Well, we will talk about it later then."

He returned slowly to the front of the room. It was not unheard of; some races had been known to interbreed. But he doubted the Others would go along with it. And what would it mean to Mothoc culture? What would the offling look like? It would have to be a male Other with a female Mothoc. Impossible. But Moc'Tor had just chastised Tarris'Kahn for not having an open mind; he could not shut the idea off without considering it.

"How serious are they about this, Tarris'Kahn?"

"Dead serious."

"You cannot truly be considering this idea, Moc'-Tor!" shouted someone.

"And why not? Do you have a better one? I know your objection. The Others are our wards. It is our responsibility to watch over them, provide for them just as we do for Etera. Our people drive deer to their hunters. We keep the waterways open. We gather flint and leave it where they can find it. We move the weather, flare the vortex to increase the harvest when we expect a harsh winter. They are unaware of our protection and care.

"Maybe what the females ask is an affront to all the males here. But remember whose fault it is that we are in this situation? We have had our way with the females for eons, never considering their wishes nor the burden of keeping them in a continual state of being seeded. And then it was us, not them, whom the Great Spirit punished with the disease that destroyed the vitality of our seed packs. Perhaps it was a message; perhaps it was the Great Spirit driving us in this direction anyway. We do not know. So to abandon any ideas out of ignorance or because they threaten our personal sensibilities is going to doom us. Is that what you prefer?"

Moc'Tor walked across the platform. "Now, who wants to meet with the females on this idea?"

"Surely they do not mean for one of the Other males to mount them? Is that not what Trestle tried and was condemned for?"

"Of course not. I do not know what they have in mind, but I do know that the Healers have ways of which we are not aware. Perhaps they already have a workable concept. Now, who will consider this idea on its merits?"

Tres'Sar's Healer, one of the few females in the group, rose to her feet. "May I speak, Moc'Tor?"

"Yes. Please state your name."

"I am Lor Onida, from Amara—the Far High Hills. I am of the Onida Healer bloodline."

Moc'Tor nodded for her to continue, taking in her small frame.

"As a Healer, I can assure you that there are ways of accomplishing this with the male Others. And as a female, I can assure you that we are, as Tarris'Kahn said, deadly serious about this solution. You males ruled over us for as long as time remembers. You showed little concern for our needs or our prefer-ences, mating us at will and assuming that one of you was the same to us as another. All the while having your own preferences about who you mounted, yet never considering we might also have preferences.

"And then you moved on to the next, never caring how shackled we might be with too many offling to care for, or how tired and worn out our bodies might be from the strain of constantly sustaining the seed you indiscriminately planted within us.

"We were created to bring life into this world. It is the right given to us, woven into the very fiber of our beings. But you can no longer give us what we need. And now that you can no longer perform your part of the process, you expect us to accept it and be punished along with you? We will not tolerate that. We are bringers of life. We serve the Great Mother; we have our own role, and we demand the right to satisfy our obligation to her as life-bringers, channels of the Aezaitera."

"But what if the Other males will not cooperate? Surely you do not expect them to—"

"Moc'Tor, so what if they will not cooperate? We need their seed, not their cooperation. Were we not taken by you males against our will for generation after generation? Bearing your offling whether we wanted to or not? But now the idea of taking what we need from a male—whether Mothoc or Other—without his consent is an affront? Please."

Moc'Tor stood in silence, amazed at the power of this small female, Lor Onida, of the Far High Hills. She had chewed up and spat out every objection they could come up with.

"No harm will come to them," she continued. "Unbeknownst to the Others, we have protected them, provided for them silently through the ages. Now we need something in return. But there is no way to ask them, no possible way of making our intentions known. Even trying to explain would terrify them."

Moc'Tor felt the energy in the room shift as cracks in long-established beliefs opened under Lor

Onida's assault. The longer he listened, the more Moc'Tor believed that her words were inspired by the Great Spirit.

The room had fallen almost silent, and Moc'Tor was about to adjourn when one last voice spoke up.

"How do you know this is the will of the Great Spirit?"

Lor Onida turned to look at the speaker. "How do you know it is not?" Her dark eyes flashed. "If we do not do this, the Mothoc will disappear from Etera entirely—as the Guardian has said himself. And then what?"

Silence.

Moc'Tor stepped forward, and all eyes shifted back to him. "It is late. I can see the weariness on your faces. We will reconvene after first light. Those of you who are willing to work with us, please stay for a moment so we can determine who we are. The others of you, I bid you good rest and thank you for your willingness to be here. Having our ideas challenged, even threatened, is uncomfortable. But if we do not change, if we do not open our thinking onto a new path, even one that goes against what we have believed so far, then our future—and I assure you it will be brief—is carved in stone. Thank you."

And Moc'Tor stepped away from the platform to await those who would join him.

At first, the pockets of those open to change were small and few. But Moc'Tor met tirelessly with each group. One wanted to focus on the process of pairing up members from the communities. They met into the early hours, discussing ways of marking and recording the pairings. Drit joined this group, and his keen mind was a rare combination of embracing both innovation and structure. Not to Moc'Tor's surprise, Oragur joined Lor Onida's group, as did many of the other Healers. Straf'Tor and his mate, Ushca, also joined. And E'ranale. Small steps, Moc'Tor kept reminding himself. Small steps will still carry us forward.

Moc'Tor let the groups continue to work together over the following day. As the day ended, they would all reconvene to hear the thoughts and ideas of the working groups.

As he walked among them, he realized that they might not think it so now, but they were the Leaders of a new age. This handful of visionaries would be the ones to guide their people through the difficult unknowns into a future of uncertainty. But at least there would be a future.

◖

At the end of the day, the Leaders of the workgroups came to speak with Moc'Tor.

Straf'Tor spoke first. "We believe we can make this work, but it will require a great deal of record keeping.

We will need a large area on which to mark the pairings. Only the wall of the Great Chamber is big enough, but it is part of our general community. We need something private, not open to everyone's eyes."

Moc'Tor nodded.

"But there is more. Even at best, with the numbers we have, we will only be able to vary our bloodlines across a few generations. Then we will be back where we are now."

"Do you have a solution?"

"We have a suggestion," Straf'Tor said.

"Speak, brother. You may not bear the title of Leader, but I recognize you as 'Tor, and I trust your wisdom."

"The two groups must work together. We must incorporate this idea of pairings with that of cross-breeding with the Others. Only if we have a complete plan will this work. We see no way around bringing the Others' seed into ours."

Moc'Tor turned to the Leader of the second group, the Healer Lor Onida.

"We agree with that," she responded. "We will work together. But we have suggestions of our own."

"Go ahead."

"The first requirement is that how we accomplish this must be confined to the Healers. There is no need for everyone to know. This is partly to control the process but also to reduce backlash. As Healers, we have a more detached view of what has to take place. We cannot trust the general population to understand."

"Who are you proposing should know?"

"Only those of us working together and moving forward; only Healers."

"I must know, Lor Onida," put in Moc'Tor. "As must some of the other Leaders. It is not just macabre curiosity about how you will accomplish it. I cannot be expected to blindly sanction this, no matter how much I trust you."

"Perhaps a small circle of Leaders, then," she reluctantly conceded. "But it must remain a closed group, Moc'Tor. Our efforts cannot stand or fall on the ground of public opinion."

"Very well, then. I support the two groups working together. Decide among yourselves what you wish to share with them. But I expect to know all your plans down to the last detail and to be kept informed as you move forward."

Both Leaders nodded and returned to join their groups.

"E'ranale, Straf'Tor, Ushca, Oragur, Drit, Dochrohan—come and find me here just before twilight. And bring Lor Onida with you."

◯

Moc'Tor sat with his small hand-picked group, those he trusted most among his community. The only stranger was Lor Onida, the strong-willed spokesperson for the females.

"I asked you to come here to discuss the need for your work to continue undisturbed, away from the eyes of the general population. And to make a proposal as to how this can be accomplished. Ours is the largest underground community in the region. Kthama stretches great lengths back into the mountain and reaches down several levels. But there is also the adjacent cavern. It is where the females reside. It shares the Mother Stream as this system does. We have always kept the genders separate, but perhaps now is the time for that to change as well. With dissent brewing between the males and females, it would serve two purposes to merge them."

"Bring the females here to live among the males?" asked E'ranale.

"Yes. There is more than enough room. It would serve two purposes. First of all, it will force us to become one community instead of being separated gender groups. Secondly, it will free up the females' dwelling for the purposes of recording. There is a separate entrance, so you will be able to control access."

"There is only one entrance?" Lor Onida asked.

"Yes. Though both share the Mother Stream, the other side enters underground and is not accessible."

Everyone but Lor Onida was nodding approval. She frowned. "This means we will have to operate from Kthama."

"We have the largest population. It makes sense," said Oragur. "And locally, there is a large village of the Others. As we go down this path, we will need to expand to the other populations, but here there is the basis for a strong start."

Lor Onida sighed and added her consent.

"Let us keep this group together for counsel," Moc'Tor suggested. "Lor Onida, are you willing to stay here, at Kthama, for a while?"

"How can I ask others to leave their community to join another if I am not willing to do so myself? I concede that it is the wisest choice."

"You are welcome to stay in my quarters," offered Oragur.

Lor Onida shot him a look that would have killed a lesser male.

"I am sorry," he hastened to say. "I meant that if you wish, I will vacate the Healer's Quarters for your use. They are spacious and have all you would need. They are also a good place for a small group to meet, if you wanted. There is more room than I require."

With the fire leaving her eyes, Lor Onida back-tracked. "That is generous of you, Oragur. I will consider it. I imagine staying in Kthama Minor would be lonely."

"Kthama Minor?" asked Moc'Tor.

Lor Onida turned to the Guardian. "I apologize. I am too headstrong; Tarris'Kahn is always reminding me. If this is the main system, then to me, this is Kthama Prime. And then it seems that the caves we will be using should be called Kthama Minor. Unless the females already named it?"

"No, it is just how it has always been," answered E'ranale. "We simply thought of it as home."

"So be it, then," approved Moc'Tor. "Once the council has disbanded, I will inform my people of the change. Dochrohan, I will need help from you and your guards to move the females across."

"They are not going to like this," said E'ranale.

"You must make them understand," Moc'Tor responded. "They are asking much of us males. Whether we are to blame for it or not, it is difficult to swallow. It is fitting that they give something in return."

"You are wise, Moc'Tor. I am blessed to be your mate."

"Do not speak too soon, female. After all this has passed, tell me if you still feel that way."

By late afternoon of the next day, Moc'Tor was in his quarters preparing to reconvene the group. He knew that while the members of the newly merged work-groups were putting their ideas and plans together, those not involved had been speaking among themselves.

"How are you feeling?" asked E'ranale.

"How am I feeling? It does not matter. All that

matters is that we keep moving forward, regardless of how difficult it is to do so."

"You are expecting trouble this afternoon?"

"Expecting it? I welcome it. All their objections must be aired here where they can be addressed, not carried back with them and nursed in dark corners to brew and fester, creating more conflict and dissent. If it appears I am dismissing or underestimating their concerns, then I must change my message." He paused. "And how are you doing?"

"I am pleased with the progress the group is making. Like you, I am prepared for a backlash from those who have not joined in."

"There are many reasons for them to have held back," Moc'Tor pointed out. "Only one of these may be disagreement with our approach. Some have more critical minds and need to be convinced of the feasibility before they will support an idea as radical as this one."

"If we can pull it off, I believe it will work. Though we will have to see how much influence the Others' seed has over the new offspring."

"Speaking of which, how exactly do you plan on making this work? Or is it too early to ask the details? And how do you know it will work."

"Oh, you already know some of the details." E'ranale gave him a conspiratorial glance.

"I do?"

"Well, yes. If you were paying attention, I think I

demonstrated the basic concept for you a couple of nights ago."

"What—?"

"What the females taught me. As I remember, you did not seem to mind what I practiced." She was toying with him now but could see his confusion was turning to anger.

"Practiced? No E'ranale. I forbid you to participate. The fact that you would even consider it—"

"I am not going to participate, Moc'Tor. I have no need or desire to do so. I want only you and our offling. I did what I did just so you would have a frame of reference. And to please you."

"But they are repulsive. Pale, small, with no covering. And what you did is so—"

"Personal? Oh, yes, it is. And as far as repulsive goes? Norcab was repulsive. As others were and are. And yes, it is unbearably personal. But do you think it any less personal to accept a male's shaft into your most intimate center, a male whose touch makes your skin crawl? Panting and straining while he slams himself into you as you grit your teeth, wishing to be anywhere else? It has taken years to learn how to put up with it, to block it out."

"The Others will not cooperate."

"They will not be awake to know. They cannot be. It would frighten them to death. As we have it planned, they will awake feeling very satisfied, with a story they can tell no one," E'ranale explained.

"How do you know they will not awake during—

Va!" Moc'Tor swore at not having the words to talk about this.

"You did not, the other night."

Moc'Tor narrowed his eyes at his mate. "E'ranale. You had better not have been toying with me, female. I may be your mate, but I am still the Adik'Tar!"

E'ranale chuckled. "Relax, Moc'Tor. I am only teasing. I did not experiment on you in that way. But some of the females have experimented on their mates. It is just a matter of administering enough tincture to knock them out long enough to collect what we need. With the Others, it will be different. At the chosen time, we will send them into a dream state. Once they are more or less asleep, let us say we will come to them in the Dream World. Except that they will see us as a maiden of the Others. It will be as real as if it were happening while they were awake, and the results will be as if they were having the real experience."

"But some Others may hear or see you. How will you handle that?"

"Simple. We do not just send those we want into the dream state; we send them all."

Moc'Tor sighed heavily. Those they want. It had not occurred to him that they might be selective, even with the Others. "One last question, and then I am done with this disturbing topic for now. After you have what you need, how will you keep them from talking about their dreams afterward?"

"This extraction process is not exactly established practice among the Others. Or us. You, yourself, were taken aback. They will have a very pleasurable and unusual dream about the attentions of an exotic maiden, and they will be too ashamed to discuss it. They are not supposed to spill their seed without procreation; it goes against all their prohibitions."

"And if you are wondering what we do once we have what we need—" E'ranale got up and came back with a little bowl of water and a small piece of clean moss, which she held up, then wadded and placed in the palm of her hand. She took a sip of water and then spat it out, soaking the little green wad and holding it up between her fingers. Then she smiled.

Moc'Tor held up his hand and walked away. "Remind me never to get on your bad side, E'ranale. You females are far too clever for me; I would never stand a chance against your inventiveness."

The Guardian left the room but stopped in the corridor just outside their quarters. He leaned his head against the wall. Was he a monster? Was this how he would be remembered—as the Leader who had brought unrest and division to his people? The Leader who had sanctioned an attack on their wards, the Others—an assault so shameful in nature that it could never be spoken about outside of closed walls? We pride ourselves on our harmonious relationship with all the Great Spirit's creatures. What would the Others think if they knew what we plan to do without their consent? And how could he condemn Trestle while approving a violation just as great though more shameful? What Trestle had nearly done was out of ignorance. What they were intending would be with full awareness of their wrongdoing.

E'ranale came up behind him. "Moc'Tor."

He was still braced against the cold stone wall, his head now cradled in his arms, and he did not look at her.

"Forgive me. I had no right to make light of it," she said. "I know that what we are about to do is a serious transgression. But in a way, they will have given their consent if they accept the maiden in the dream," she offered.

"That is true, as far as it goes, but they will not have given their consent to have their essences used to seed our females." Moc'Tor's voice was muffled against the wall.

"They are gentle and kind. They would help us if we asked."

"Yes, but we cannot ask. We have no shared language, and we virtually never make contact with them." He paused before continuing. "If I cannot convince the leadership waiting back in the meeting room that this is the right course, the only course, then how am I to convince the males of the general population?"

"You have said, so many times, Moc'Tor, that you are the Leader. You do not need to convince the general population. Nor do you need their permission. They do not have to know the details, and it is best that way.

"As for the leadership, they need to join with you and put their personal reservations aside. If we are to avoid extinction, we have two paths only, and we will have to go down both of them simultaneously in order to survive," she added.

Moc'Tor finally turned and met her gaze. "It is time. Walk with me."

As before, guards stood near the entrance to the meeting room, ensuring that passers-by could not be within earshot of the proceedings. As it was, curiosity, concern, and tension were at an all-time high.

Moc'Tor began speaking without waiting for the conversation to die down, and immediately the room fell silent.

"We are here tonight to finalize our plans for moving forward. The groups who volunteered to work out the initial details of the two possible approaches have joined to create one collective effort. I ask the original two Leaders to join me now." He signaled for Lor Onida and his brother, Straf'Tor, to join him.

"Before we give you our report, are there any lingering objections that we need to air?" asked Straf'Tor.

E'ranale looked at him as he stood next to his brother, her mate. Straf'Tor had a dark coat, but they were almost identical in build and structure. A sadness swept over her, realizing that she might be looking at the last of their kind—the last pure strain of Mothoc.

Tarris'Kahn rose to speak. "We have talked about your proposals, Moc'Tor. We are ready to hear what the workgroups have to report before we make any comments of our own."

Moc'Tor nodded to his brother to continue.

"As Moc'Tor has explained," Straf'Tor began, "we have combined the efforts of both groups. Those of us working out how to plan pairings between young adults as they mature—well, we quickly discovered that while this is an excellent option, our limited numbers might bring us back to this exact point in several generations. After the sickness, we simply do not have the numbers to spread our seed widely enough. So there is no choice for us; we must bring in new seed or perish altogether. That may not be the news you want to hear, but it is the truth."

Lor Onida added, "We will not go into the details, but our plan for crossbreeding with the Others has been well-thought-out. If we do it as planned, the damage to our relationship with the Others will be minimal or nonexistent."

The Leaders looked at each other.

"If you do not mind our asking—" An unidentified male spoke up.

"I do mind. I understand your natural curiosity, but what we will be doing is best kept between those directly involved. I know we have not earned your trust in this matter, which makes it harder for you to accept."

"The Others will know eventually," added the same male.

"Perhaps. But we only rarely have direct contact with them. Generations ahead, they may figure it out when the effects of their seed line are showing in us. But by then, the crossbreeding will be firmly established and completed."

"It is the end of us."

Lor Onida ignored him and continued. "Those in your communities who are producing healthy offspring will continue as they have been. Any female who has had a deadborn will be offered the chance to participate in our plan. Once we have it working, we will move to other communities and share our knowledge so they can do the same. If we are smart, if we are swift, if we are wise, within a few generations we will be far enough down the path that leads away from extinction."

Moc'Tor surveyed the room. He could read their reactions even if his male seventh sense hadn't been able to gauge their state of receptiveness. About half were convinced. Another quarter or so were still not committed either way, and the last quarter was mostly against it but for reasons having to do with the males' further loss of control. The Others are our wards. We have always protected them, looked after them without their knowledge. If there were any other way—

Moc'Tor took the floor once more. "You have heard from both workgroup Leaders. They will continue to work on their plan. As they said, once it is perfected, they will come to your communities and work with you and your people, if that is what you wish. I do not expect you to embrace this idea enthusiastically. But without your support, we will fail. It will require our collective effort to bring it about.

"This is not a tale to be told to offling at night to entertain them," he continued. "This is our reality. We change, or we die off. Forever. The choice and the power are in your hands. Once you leave here, it will be up to you which path you lead your own people down. But the truth is we cannot afford to lose the support of any of you. Our numbers are so low that we now need every one of our people if we are to survive. But I also cannot force you to participate."

The Leader walked down into the audience, intentionally heading toward the pocket where he had observed the most resistance. "You are all-powerful Leaders. Many of you said at the start that your people look to you for answers, but you know that the answers are not always easy. Sometimes we can soften them, but this is not one of those times. This will be difficult. You will meet resistance from members of your communities, just as I have met resistance from many of you.

"Before behavior can change, the thinking behind it must change. When you go back, remember your own process, your own struggle with this. And consider the alternatives. You can go back and help them understand that this is a solution, a path forward, and then work with us. Not an easy solution, no. Not one to be proud of. But there is one.

"Or you can go back and tell them there is a solution, but that you do not support it. You owe it to your communities at least to let them know there is a way forward. And to give them time to adjust. If you do less than that, you are not a Leader; you are but a tyrant who uses lies as a shield to protect himself from conflict. They deserve to know the truth, and they deserve to hear it from you."

The room was quiet; Moc'Tor's words hung in the air. E'ranale felt the spirit move in her, and she knew she must speak to the group. She caught Oragur's eye and stepped forward, cueing him to stand beside her as a Healer and also as a male.

"I do not understand what it is like to be male," she began. "I do not pretend to bear your burdens or face your struggles. I do know that you have been taxed considerably over the past decades. And to hear what we are planning only adds to the weight you carry. The idea of our females, your females, using another's seed is no doubt repugnant to you.

"However, it is not too long ago that you openly shared us, not caring how many of you mated us or whose seed ripened in whose belly. This is not so different. But if you still struggle with what lies ahead, try to remember, this is not our choice. This is not something we choose willingly.

"We would never ordinarily seek out the males of the Others. You are our males. You are the ones we desire and long for. You are the ones in our hearts and the ones with whom we share our beds, our bodies, and our lives. We do not wish in any way to replace you. We can never replace you; we only wish for our people to survive, and therefore we must fill our purpose to produce offling for ourselves and for you. Offling for us all to raise as sons and daughters of our people. Nothing more. You will always be those around whom we build our lives. The rest will pass into history and be forgotten, just as the waters of the Great River flow downstream and disappear from view. If we do not take this path, the Mothoc and our responsibilities and gifts to Etera will cease. Consider those consequences. Which is the path you can most easily live with?"

E'ranale exhaled and released her tension. In her heart, she felt they had done all they could. Whatever happened next, it was out of their hands.

CHAPTER 8

Akar'Tor had not left as Khon'Tor had told him to do. He returned to his quarters accompanied by the two guards, where he sulked, trying to figure out how he could force Khon'Tor to accept his presence. He knew that his father, Haan, was with the others at the High Council meeting. He knew enough from stories his mother had told him that they were a higher authority, higher than Khon'Tor. He wondered if he might appeal to them and if they could force Khon'Tor to let him stay.

I have nothing to lose. Khon'Tor has made it plain that he does not want me around. I have to be smarter about it. But if I appeal to the High Council, they can force him to let me stay. And then he cannot harm me without their finding out. Surely that is against their laws, just as it is against ours. If Mother were here, that is what she would tell me to do.

Once I am allowed to stay, I can work on showing Tehya just how much better off she would be with me than with Khon'Tor. How much better off they all *would be. He said I am not a prisoner, so let us see if that is true.*

Akar'Tor got up and left, the guards following behind him. When he came to the main junction, he asked one of the guards, "Where is the High Council meeting? Take me there."

They had not been told not to speak with him, only to keep track of him and so the taller of the two answered, "We do not have permission to take you anywhere. We are to follow you."

"Very well, I will find it myself if I have to go down every corridor there is." And he set out to do just that.

It took a while, but he eventually found the room where the Leaders were meeting. He pushed open the stone door and stepped inside.

Once again, Acaraho's pressure on Khon'Tor's shoulder kept him seated, but nothing could keep Khon'Tor's eyes from searing into Akar'Tor as he walked into the room.

"You are interrupting." Haan turned to address his son, speaking quickly and forgetting to add Handspeak to his spoken words.

"I have come to apologize," he said, looking up at the Sarnonn who had raised him and who was the only father he had ever known. "May I please address the High Council?"

Out of the corner of his eye, Kurak'Kahn could see Khon'Tor bristling. But he had no grounds to refuse a direct request to be heard.

"Announce yourself and proceed," the Overseer ordered.

"I am Akar'Tor, son of Khon'Tor, who is Leader of the People of the High Rocks, and Hakani, his Third Rank. I was raised among the Sarnonn as you call them. Haan here, Leader of the Sassen, raised me. He is the only father I have ever known. But as you can see, I am not one of the Sarnonn. Earlier, I interrupted Khon'Tor to ask for a place here as his acknowledged heir. That was wrong of me. I came to apologize for my actions."

Akar's performance did not fool Kurak'Kahn. The upstart had shown his true nature earlier. He had not *asked* for anything, only demanded. Kurak'Kahn was sorry to see that Akar'Tor appeared to have inherited both his parents' false natures.

"Is it not to us that you need to apologize, Akar'-Tor," said Kurak'Kahn.

Akar'Tor bit his lip and turned to face Khon'Tor. "I apologize for my actions earlier. I would like to request to live here at Kthama. I would like to learn the ways of the People in hopes of finding my place among them."

Khon'Tor's fists tightened and his jaw clenched as he stared at Akar'Tor without blinking. Tehya was sitting directly at Khon'Tor's side, and he sat silent, with his eyes locked on Akar's, waiting for even the tiniest look in Tehya's direction.

And then it came, the most fleeting of glances at Tehya—but it was enough for Khon'Tor.

Khon'Tor flew to his feet.

"Denied. Return to your home among the Sarnonn and your mother. Hakani has no rank here, and there is no place for you, either. And I certainly do not have the time or inclination to make one for you."

Adia closed her eyes and shook her head.

With his back to the rest of the High Council, Akar'Tor returned Khon'Tor's glare. However, he masked his hostility as he turned to address Kurak'Kahn.

"You can see that I am not welcome at Kthama, but as Khon'Tor's offspring, I have a right here. I appeal to you to override my blood father's rejection of me and allow me to stay. If I understand the situation, there is no heir to Khon'Tor's leadership."

"There is none *as yet*," interjected Khon'Tor, moving to stand between Akar'Tor and the High Council Overseer.

"I stand corrected," he replied. "But at best, it will be years and years before any offspring you produce will be ready to take over. And there is no guarantee you will produce another male."

A difficult situation for Khon'Tor, thought Kurak'Kahn. *Akar'Tor is wrong. There is a male heir,*

Nootau, by Adia. Only, Khon'Tor cannot claim him without revealing his violation of Adia to everyone. Adia removed her accusation against Khon'Tor, tying our hands, but that does not solve the problem of his crime in the eyes of our people should it come to light. And I doubt his young mate, Tehya, knows any of that, nor does Khon'Tor want her to.

"Time is dragging. I call a recess for the rest of the day. Akar'Tor, son of Hakani, you must leave; the matter will not be resolved here and now. If we see a need for your return, we will call for you," said Kurak'Kahn.

The attendees rose to leave. As they filtered out, Kurak'Kahn approached Khon'Tor. "A word if I may," he said. "Alone."

Khon'Tor turned to Acaraho, glanced at Akar'Tor, and then back to Acaraho, "Please see to it that Tehya gets safely back to our quarters, or wherever else she wishes to go."

Once alone, Khon'Tor addressed the Overseer. "If you think you can pressure me to accept that insolent *Quat*, you are wasting your time, Overseer."

"I understand your position. Perhaps better than you realize. But your approach with Akar'Tor is neither effective nor beneficial to your cause. Clearly, you do not want him here. But he is not going to drop it, and he does have a claim."

"A claim? Based on what? An ill-fated pairing between his mother and me? A relationship that never should have happened, consisting only of years of bitterness and hostility? He was conceived in hatred, Kurak'Kahn, *that* is his birthright—not to be any kind of a Leader here."

"I am now speaking to you as one male to another, Khon'Tor. If you use this tactic, you will lose. Perhaps everything. Maybe not right away, but down the road."

Khon'Tor scoffed. "Why are you helping me? The last time I faced you, you wished to banish me."

"I believe your Healer set us all straight on that. What you did was an abomination. But your Healer is smarter and wiser than all of us. She recognizes that your people need you; all the People need you. If she can set aside what you did to her for the collective sake of the People, then so can I. But you are not invincible, and right now, you have two great weaknesses—Tehya and Akar'Tor. Clearly, you cannot control your reactions to Akar'Tor. And as long as that is the case, he holds the real power between the two of you."

"And how will having him here help me with that?"

"What is the most dangerous enemy?" asked Kurak'Kahn.

"The one you cannot see coming," Khon'Tor answered. "You are saying I should let him come live here. Mentor him, even?"

"As it stands now, there is only one outcome to the path you are on. Either you will kill him, or he will kill you. But before that happens, a great deal of damage can be done," said Kurak'Kahn.

"If killing him is an option, I can save us all a great deal of trouble and take care of that right now." Khon'Tor ran his hand through his silver crown. He paused before continuing.

"Kurak'Kahn. I cannot have him around Tehya."

Silence.

"For many reasons."

"I understand. But you cannot make him go away, either—not yet —and you cannot win by taking him head-on because it makes no sense to those who do not know the rest of the story. It only makes you appear reactive, jealous, small. You must outsmart him. Eventually, he will make a mistake—"

"You are saying either a mistake that will prove him unfit for leadership or a mistake that gives me cause rightfully to banish him from Kthama," Khon'Tor replied.

"Yes. You can protect Tehya. Assign a hundred guards if you must, with orders to never let him anywhere near her. Send him out into the fields and task him with learning the skills all offspring are expected to master. The fall planting season is coming. Show him how much he does not know. Tear down his arrogance and confidence. He is young and brash as we all once were. And he has the disadvantage of his mother's manipulative, deceitful character behind him. Haan seems of good character, and it is too bad that did not transfer to Akar'Tor in his upbringing."

Khon'Tor almost chuckled at the thought of Akar'Tor toiling in the fields with the young offspring, bent over planting row after row of Goldenseal root under the hot sun.

"Thank you for your help, Overseer."

"I do not know what you are talking about. This conversation never took place. All I did was ask where you got that beautiful necklace that Tehya wears. I believe my mate would favor one."

Khon'Tor smiled. "Oh'Dar made it for her. Next time he returns, I will ask him if he would make one for your mate."

"Thank you, Khon'Tor. I know it would please her greatly."

Khon'Tor remained in the room after Kurak'Kahn left. He sat and held his head in his hands. *Two enemies are now allies; Acaraho and the Overseer. And Kurak'Kahn is right. He is right in everything he said. But nothing alarms me more than having Akar here. Before, when I had nothing to lose, I was invincible. All I cared about was my position as Leader, and I knew how to defend that.*

Now, the thought of losing Tehya is unbearable. My love for her distracts me, makes me vulnerable. I must do whatever it takes to ensure she is safe, protected—even if she objects. Only then will I be able to do as Kurak'Kahn said, create the stage for Akar to make a mistake big enough to warrant his expulsion—or worse.

He has all my best and worst attributes—it will be a lot like battling myself, only a younger version without my years of experience. But the conflict between Akar and me, what effect will that have on our relationship with Haan, should it come to—

My thoughts are all over the place. Time to find Tehya and get some rest.

CHAPTER 9

The wedding plans were set. Shadow Ridge was decorated as never before. White fabric draped the entrance and the fencing leading up to the drive. Jenkins' men had built an arbor and whitewashed it. The women had woven ribbons around the frame and were going to add flowers when the day came, creating a beautiful setting for the ceremony.

There wouldn't be many in attendance, but that was how Jenkins and Mrs. Morgan wanted it. Oh'Dar would be standing with Jenkins as his 'Best Man'—a term which indicated a close relationship between the two of them, as Jenkins explained to Oh'Dar. Mrs. Thomas would stand with Mrs. Morgan. Oh'Dar smiled as he watched the joyful activity around the ranch.

That morning, as he was leaving the stables and heading inside to change, a carriage drove up carrying a single passenger. Oh'Dar stopped dead in his tracks as the delicate and graceful figure of Miss Blain stepped out.

Oh'Dar walked briskly over and extended her a hand, which she took, assuming it was the cab driver helping her. When she finally turned to thank him, she caught her breath, finding herself staring straight into the blue eyes of the most handsome man she'd ever seen.

"Grayson," she blurted out before she could catch herself.

"At your service, Miss Blain," he said and gave a small bow. "I'm glad you could make it. You're as beautiful as ever."

She blushed at his compliment, her hand still resting in his.

"I'm very happy for Mrs. Morgan and Mr. Jenkins. As I'm sure you are too—Master Grayson."

"I am. Of course, none of it would have happened had they not finally admitted their feelings for each other. Would it, Miss Blain?"

"Of course not," she stammered. "Nothing could have turned out better—for them, I mean."

Oh'Dar signaled for the driver to bring her bags to the top of the stairs.

"You no doubt wish to get settled. I believe they've prepared your old room on the off chance that you might arrive," he explained.

"Yes, thank you. I know the way. Thank you, Master Grayson," she said and scurried off.

He's changed. He's so self-assured—and those eyes. Oh, why did I come? I knew he'd be here. He's definitely no longer, in any way, a boy.

🌀

Oh'Dar couldn't help watching Miss Blain climb the steps to the front door where Mrs. Thomas was waiting. Though his trip back to Kthama had reminded him that it would always be his home, he hadn't made up his mind in which world he belonged. Or to which woman his heart belonged, either.

He dressed carefully for the ceremony, putting on the new clothes that his grandmother had purchased just for this occasion. With his straight black hair and vibrant blue eyes, the new black jacket, pants, and boots heightened his striking looks. He'd learned to see himself through Waschini eyes and knew he was what they considered attractive. As he looked in the mirror, he wondered if Acise could see him like this, would she find him handsome in the White man's clothes? *That's odd; I'd have thought I would be thinking about Miss Blain.*

Oh'Dar pulled the jacket down on his shoulders as Jenkins had taught him. *Perhaps when I go back, I will ask Honovi about a black dye and make some dark wrappings like this for home.* As he thought about Kthama, the old feelings of homesickness stirred.

I'd better snap out of it. I've just got back here; I can't leave again so soon. Besides, before I return, I want to

*spend some of the allowance that Grandmother gives me.
I have some gifts in mind that I know Honovi, Nadiwani,
Tehya, and my mother would love. And Acise.*

Oh'Dar made his last adjustments and headed
downstairs, where others had started gathering. The
gentleman performing the ceremony was someone
from the local town whom Oh'Dar had never seen
before. There were many people in attendance
whom Oh'Dar had never met.

Before long, Jenkins took his place under the
arbor with Oh'Dar standing next to him. Across from
them stood Mrs. Thomas and seated in the front row
was Miss Blain. Out of the corner of his eye, he could
see her glancing at him.

Shortly, Mrs. Morgan came walking up toward
where they were standing. Oh'Dar was struck with
how beautiful she was, her auburn hair done up on
top of her head with flowers across the front. Before
long, the gentleman finished speaking. Oh'Dar
watched as Jenkins took his grandmother's hand and
pushed the gold ring onto her finger. They
exchanged a brief kiss, and a large clamor of
applause rose from those in attendance.

The rest of the afternoon consisted of talking and
eating. Oh'Dar enjoyed seeing the ladies in all their
different clothing—more ornate than any he'd seen
before. It gave him ideas that he was anxious to share
with Tehya.

When Miss Blain came up beside him, Oh'Dar
was lingering near the long table, which was laid out

with delicious food. She picked up some fruit without looking at him. "Your grandmother looks beautiful today, Master Grayson. It is good to see her so happy."

"It is indeed, Miss Blain. So, what are your plans; will you be in town long?" Oh'Dar surprised himself by how well he'd learned to mimic their different styles of speaking, sometimes more relaxed, sometimes more distant and formal, as they called it, depending on the setting.

"I came in to conduct some business. I'm glad the timing worked out so I could be here for them today."

"Well. Miss Blain, I hope you enjoy your time here. Let me know if there is anything I can do to make your stay more pleasant." Oh'Dar walked away, not wanting to monopolize her time.

Mrs. Morgan, now Mrs. Jenkins, and her new husband didn't leave on any type of a honeymoon. Oh'Dar noticed that the evening of their ceremony, everyone stayed outside well into the early hours, enjoying a bonfire that Mr. Jenkins' farmhands had built.

Mrs. Thomas explained to Oh'Dar that it had something to do with giving them their privacy. The People's offspring weren't taught about mating until it was time for them to be paired. They were kept ignorant in an attempt to control indiscriminate pairing and avoid experimentation. Oh'Dar didn't know the finer details of what was going on between his grandmother and Jenkins, and it caused him no end of questions.

I need someone to explain this to me. I'm well past pairing age, and I only know the basics. I remember carrying Acise to the sleeping mat as if I knew what I was doing, so perhaps it is all something that comes naturally when the moment is at hand. But there has to be more to it than that. I want to know how to be good at it.

The next few days were spent with the ranch hands and the other help orchestrating Jenkins' move into the main house. Oh'Dar helped where he could. Before long, they shared their first breakfast together, with Jenkins settled in with them, all under the same roof.

Because she was now Mrs. Jenkins and no longer Mrs. Morgan, and everyone kept forgetting the fact, she asked her new husband how he'd feel if everyone at the ranch started referring to her as Miss Vivian. Jenkins had no problem with this, and so, from then on, Miss Vivian it was, unless there was company.

Miss Vivian looked up from her morning tea. Oh'Dar thought she looked particularly relaxed since she and Jenkins had gotten married.

"Marriage suits you, Grandmother. You look happy and relaxed."

Jenkins chuckled as he took a drink of his

morning coffee, smiling at his new bride over the lip of the cup.

Blushing, she replied, "Thank you, Grayson. Now, have you decided your plans for the future? Are you returning to the hospital for more schooling, or are you going to ask Dr. Miller to take you on as an apprentice?"

"I'd like to go into town and talk to Dr. Miller. I also have a little shopping to do while I'm there."

"That's interesting. Something for Miss Blain, perhaps?"

"No. I believe she left town already, Grand-mother. I don't know that I will ever see her again."

"I don't mean to get personal, Grayson, but you were so smitten with her at one time. Has that changed?"

Oh'Dar sighed. "It is a hopeless cause, Grand-mother. She does not even live near here. And my path is still uncertain. I've chalked it up to, what was it you called it, Jenkins, a young man's fancy? What-ever that is." He laughed. "But I did enjoy flirting with her. No doubt about that."

He put down his own cup of tea for which he'd developed a liking. "I just wish someone would explain to me how mating works, so I'd know what I'm supposed to do when the time comes."

Jenkins just about spat out his coffee.

"Grayson!" Miss Vivian brought her napkin up to partially cover her face.

Jenkins put down his cup and pushed back his chair.

"Alright, son," he said, looking at his bride and suppressing a chuckle. "It's time you and I had a little talk. Come with me."

Oh'Dar tossed his own napkin on top of his plate and got up to go with Jenkins. As they left, Mrs. Thomas and Miss Vivian were blushing, but smiling at each other.

"Oh," said Oh'Dar sometime later after Jenkins had finished explaining the basics of what took place during mating, apparently called making love.

"Oh? That's all you can say?" chided Jenkins.

"No. I mean, thank you, but I already understood the basics. I just feel stupid. I get how the pieces fit together, but how do I make it pleasurable for her?"

"Don't feel stupid, Grayson. Did your father not explain this to you?"

"No, he didn't. He would have eventually, I mean, there is a time when it's explained to those who are old enough to pair up, it is called the Ashwea Tare —" Oh'Dar stopped midsentence, realizing what he'd done.

"Grayson, I'm so sorry. I should not have asked. I know you're protecting whoever it was who cared for you all those years. I didn't mean to pry."

Oh'Dar put his head in his hands. "I can't live like

this. Split between all these worlds. It is too hard. I want to tell you and Grandmother about my past, but I don't dare. There is no way you could understand any of it without seeing for yourselves, and I can't do that. It has nothing to do with you. It is one of our Sacred Laws, and it is there for good reason."

Stop talking, Oh'Dar, he scolded himself.

"It does not matter where I am, here with you, or there with them, I always feel I should be in the other place. But I have to choose. Please, teach me the family business. I need to try to fit in here because I can't bear to leave Grandmother again. Perhaps if I knew more, it would help me make peace with staying at Shadow Ridge."

"I will be more than glad to teach you anything you want to know, son. But it sounds as if you're trying to force yourself to make a decision you're not ready to make."

"I have to choose, don't you see? I'm just hurting everyone by bouncing back and forth like this."

"Grayson, I'm going to be very blunt with you. What you're talking about can't be done. You'll never have peace if you use your will to make a decision your heart has the final say on. You have to take it one day at a time. Eventually, something will happen that will settle it for you. And when it does, you will know what you want. I promise; you will know."

"I want to believe you. I want to believe there will be an end to this torment."

"You know that I've no idea who these other

people are, Grayson. But I know they must love you just as much as we do. And anyone who loves someone ultimately wants them to be happy. Your grandmother wouldn't want you to stay here if you weren't content here. As much as it would hurt her if you left permanently, I promise you, she'd understand. All she wants in the world for you is to be happy. And I'm sure your other people, whoever they are, feel the same way."

What*ever they are would be more accurate*, Oh'Dar thought bitterly. *It is an impossible dream, but how I wish I could take them there, blend these two worlds of mine together. Then perhaps I could be at rest.*

"Thank you for talking to me, Jenkins. It helps me understand some of the things that have been going on in my body since I've been around Miss Blain and the —other females. Maybe it is something you just have to experience for yourself. I hope when my time comes, I'll know what to do. I've overheard the males—the men—saying it is the male—man's—responsibility to make the fe—woman want to come to him. They seem to spend a fair amount of time flirting and teasing."

"We can talk about it more whenever you're ready, Grayson. Some of it will come naturally, but yes, there are some things you can do to make it better for her. Just let me know. Oh, and by the way, I think it's time you started calling me Ben." He patted Oh'Dar on the shoulder and left him to himself.

As Jenkins walked away, he thought, *That's an*

interesting philosophy and quite wise, but peculiar how he talks about them as the males. *I wonder if those* males *have any tricks we don't know about.* He chuckled.

○

Later that evening, while Jenkins and Miss Vivian were lying together quietly, he told her about the conversation in the stalls.

"I tried to explain to Grayson what happens during lovemaking. I slipped up and asked him if his father hadn't told him anything about sex. He started answering and said no, but that when the males were old enough to mate, they were taught about it in some type of ritual. He had a name for it, but I was so shocked he was talking about his past that I didn't catch it."

Miss Vivian shook her head. "I don't know what the secrecy is about—but I know we must respect it. It is obvious he was raised by the Locals. I don't know why it has to be such a mystery. Perhaps he fears some retribution will come to them for taking him in."

"I don't know. I remember you said that they did speak with one of the tribes in the area; well anyway, they talked to them but found no sign of Grayson. It is possible that he was taken away to another village, or maybe they just hid him very well. Either way, there is nothing we can do about it until he decides to open up."

"I wonder why he does not trust us," she said.

"He said that they had Sacred Laws about contact with us—Outsiders, he said. I don't think it is us personally. I'd say he wants us to know, or he wouldn't be as torn up about it as he is."

Miss Vivian snuggled up against her new husband. "I'm just glad he's home. I hope this time it is to stay."

Jenkins reached over and turned off the gas lamp without answering. What he wanted to tell her was not to get her hopes up. *Anyone who struggles so hard to stay in one place will one day tire of the battle. Grayson's will may be strong, but in the end, it is the desires of the heart that eventually prevail.*

CHAPTER 10

The strain of having their long-established beliefs challenged was showing on everyone in the High Council meeting. Times were hard enough without Haan pulling the foundation of their history out from under them by telling them they were not the product of cross-breeding between the Sarnonn and the Brothers, but of the Mothoc and the Brothers.

Khon'Tor was not sure how much more he could take, either. He had lost touch with everything else going on at Kthama. He was grateful for the dedication of Mapiya, Awan, and all the others who were keeping the machine of life in motion at Kthama. Meals were provided, refuse removed, questions answered around the clock. By the time they got back to their quarters, everyone was too tired to do anything except sleep. As much as Khon'Tor wanted the release of mating Tehya at the end of the day, he knew she was just as tired as he was and would not press her to accept him.

Instead, they cuddled.

Tehya curled up against him in her favorite position, head resting in the crook of his shoulder, and her arm splayed across him so she could play with the mass of thick hair on his chest. The strength and protection promised by his hard muscles comforted her. His strong heartbeat and the rise and fall of his breathing lulled her into half-sleep. She had learned not to throw her leg over his front, though this was her preferred position, as it proved too provocative, and she did not want to arouse him only to refuse him—though she never *had* refused him.

As she dozed, she wondered what would happen if she did turn him away. Part of their playfulness was based on his ordering her around. She liked that he took charge. She found she enjoyed surrendering to his orders, though everything he had ever done was always for her pleasure. She had no fear of him whatsoever, despite the times he was curt with her—which, come to think of it, seemed to be increasing in frequency. Occasionally, Hakani's words of warning entered her mind, but she extinguished them immediately. The female was bitter and not to be trusted. *She would do anything to hurt Khon'Tor, and she would not be above using me to do it.*

She buried her fingers deeper in his curly dark chest covering.

I am glad he is sleeping. The strain of everything is showing on him. And now there is the problem of Akar'-Tor. Why does he insist on joining us? I can understand that he does not fit in with the Sarnonn, but he does not know us, either. He would do just as well to ask to join another community. I do not know how he can possibly think he would be qualified to replace a male such as Khon'Tor. Ever. I hope he does not stay. I do not like how he looks at me.

💫

Haan stood outside Kthama, looking up at the array of stars blanketing the night sky. He wondered how Hakani was doing with their daughter. *What will become of Kalli? She will be an outsider, the same as Akar'Tor. Though she will be part of our community, it is obvious she is mixed. It is clear our males cannot mate with their females. But our only other choice is to hope that the Akassa will help us. It is time I bring it up. I have already broken the contract. Whatever harm I have brought to them by my acts of desperation is already in motion and cannot be stopped.*

💫

The next morning, Acaraho found Khon'Tor and Tehya and swung his leg over the bench to sit with them.

"I would ask how you slept, but if you are always as tired as I am, I already know the answer," remarked Acaraho.

"Yes. Sleeping is not a problem. And we need to talk."

"I agree—all of us. Perhaps before the next assembly?" suggested Acaraho.

"Yes. Please make the arrangements," said Khon'Tor.

Acaraho nodded.

After they had eaten, Acaraho gathered everyone in their usual meeting room. Acaraho, Adia, Nadi-wani, Tehya, and Awan sat in the meeting circle and waited for Khon'Tor to begin.

"We have not met since the High Council meeting started. A lot has happened. I need each of you to check in. Status updates, observations, concerns. Awan? Acaraho? "

"Food stores are holding up. Nothing to worry about as far as the operation of Kthama goes. The watchers report no troublesome outside activity. By troublesome, I mean anything unusual—Waschini, Sarnonn, and sorry to bring it up, but I am glad to say, no sign of Hakani. So as far as outside threats to our people go, there is nothing to report."

Awan nodded his agreement.

Khon'Tor repeated. "Anyone else?"

Everyone shook their heads.

"I have nothing, Khon'Tor," Adia said. "But what

Acaraho was alluding to, and what is on all our minds, is Akar'Tor."

"You should all know that I have decided to let him stay."

Troubled glances circled among those in the room.

"That surprises me," said Nadiwani, who was usually silent.

"I understand, Khon'Tor," said Acaraho.

"I will also have to let Haan know that I am letting Akar stay. I want him under watch at all times. I do not care how you do it. I do not care if he knows or not. And I do not want him anywhere near Tehya or our quarters. Awan, regarding Tehya, I cannot make it clear enough that the highest priority is her safety. Do whatever it takes. You cannot make a mistake when it comes to the means you use to protect her. Do I make myself clear on this?"

Awan replied, "Yes, Adik'Tar."

"Do not confuse my allowing him to join us with any recognition of his claim to the leadership of the People of the High Rocks. I do not care whose blood is in his veins. Akar'Tor will never lead Kthama. I will kill him before I allow that."

"What will he do while he is here?"

"I want him trained in everything we do. Starting with fall planting and harvest. Helping the females in the kitchen. Repairs. Whatever you can think of."

Adia and Nadiwani looked at each other and smiled.

"Not quite the warrior's training he is expecting, Khon'Tor," said Adia.

"He who wishes to lead must first be willing to serve. Akar has many hard lessons coming, I believe."

Then Khon'Tor changed the subject. "I believe Haan has a request of some sort coming our way. I am still not convinced that Hakani's seeding was not an experiment. An ignorant and dangerous one, and yet on some level a calculated risk. On the other hand, I do not think he would knowingly put her in harm's way. Clearly, their Healer, whoever that is, was not equipped to deal with either Akar's sickness or her condition, since they sought us out."

He let out a heavy breath. "Alright. Prepare to go back in. Keep your eyes and ears open. Acaraho, give me a report as soon as you and Awan have worked out the details about Akar and Tehya. That is all."

They trickled out of the room and made their way on to the next meeting. Khon'Tor caught Kurak'Kahn before it officially started.

"I do not know how much longer Haan's story is going to continue, but perhaps it is time to discuss our own challenges. It might speed other information to the forefront."

"I agree. Everyone looks strained and exhausted."

Kurak'Kahn took back control of the meeting

from Haan. "Let me recap the focus of our coming together, though this is still connected to what you have been telling us, Haan. The majority of us in this group met nearly a full year ago because we were facing serious problems with our population. We are running out of combinations for our pairings. It is just a matter of time before our offspring will start showing defects.

"At that time, I asked each of you to send out scouts to try to find other populations of our people or even of yours, Haan—though we did not truly think you were still in the area. Perhaps in the far regions, but not here, so close. We do not have any easy choices. If we cannot find other communities of our own kind, then we face extinction unless we find a way to introduce a new—factor—into our bloodline.

"Because of Haan's story, we know that we are not the result of his people breeding with the Brothers, but of the Mothoc, the Fathers-Of-Us-All, as he calls them. Our Ancients? I can see it no other way than that our challenge is the same one they faced long ago, and our choices are just as hard. Because our blood is already mingled with the Brothers, that path is probably no longer open to us. The last time we met, we thought we had a single path forward. Now that we know the Sarnonn still walk among us, we have an alternate direction to consider."

Adia thought of Hakani's offspring, a product of the Sarnonn and the People. *Our choices are physical strength and longevity with the Sarnonn or dexterity and innovation with the Waschini. It would be far easier with the Sarnonn, but*—Adia caught herself in her own prejudice, realizing she saw breeding with the Sarnonn as a step backward.

Kurak'Kahn turned to Haan, and bluntly asked, "Is that not also why you are here, Haan?"

Haan stood up. "I am here because Khon'Tor asked me to share my knowledge of our past with you. But yes, Overseer, I do need the help of the People. I came to Kthama seeking aid for Akar'Tor and Hakani, who was carrying my offling. I would not have sought you out otherwise. But once the contact was made, I realized you might be willing to help us in another way. We have the same problem that you do. Our numbers are too few, and our bloodlines too close. We will have to stop reproducing within a few generations or risk the same defects in our offling that you mentioned."

"You have only a few generations?"

Adia spoke up. "Overseer, we estimate that the Sarnonn may live two to three times as long as we do. So Haan's meaning of the term *generations* is not within the same timeframe as ours. So his two generations could easily be as much as eight of ours. And the Mothoc lived far longer than that. Probably, our breeding with the Brothers shortened our lifespans.

"We still do not understand, Haan. If the Mothoc bred with the Brothers, why are your people and our people still walking Etera together?"

"The Akassa did not replace the Sassen. The Akassa and Sassen walked together with the Fathers for many generations. The Fathers-Of-Us-All created two paths; Akassa and Sassen. And they created the Laws before we Sassen left the Mothoc communities."

Through the upcoming years, the Mothoc females gave birth to more and more cross-bred offling. Knowing that the process worked, the two Healers, Lor Onida and her mate, Oragur, traveled to the other Mothoc communities with local populations of Others and taught the process they had devised. As far as they were aware, the Others did not know what the Mothoc were doing. To begin with, the Mothoc had seldom interacted with the Others, and in time, if the Others became aware of the Mothoc's altered appearance, they might never make a connection between that and the past.

The first two generations of cross-breeding had produced offling still very much like the Mothoc. As the second generation was again crossed with the Others' seed, the Others' influence started to come to the forefront. As the years passed, each subsequent generation was bred as soon as possible. Eventually, there were two distinct new seed lines living at Kthama; those who resembled the Mothoc more—the Sassen—and those who had more of the Others' influence—who would become known as the Akassa.

As their population became stable, the sense of urgency faded, and unrest stirred among the two factions across all the communities—almost in unison.

Centuries later, the Great Chamber and corridors of Kthama were once again full of life. Moc'Tor still ruled with E'ranale by his side, but his subsequent generations of offling and those of his brother, Straf'-Tor, had taken very different paths. Moc'Tor continued to pursue the introduction of the Others' bloodline, whereas Straf'Tor was steadfast that they dare not dilute the original Mothoc blood any further. The differences in ideology were creating dissent.

"Oragur and Lor Onida believe the differences will now be self-sustaining," said E'ranale to her mate.

"Meaning?"

"Meaning that those who wish to breed with others of their kind inside the community will produce offling true to their parents. We no longer need to introduce the Others' seed into our females for the changes to be handed down."

Moc'Tor breathed a sigh of relief. "How is this one doing?" he asked E'ranale, placing his hand on her swollen belly.

"She is quieter than the others. There is a sense of peace about her."

"Her? How can you know it is a female?"

"I do not know. But I strongly feel that she is."

"Have you thought of a name?"

"Yes. If you approve, I would like to name her Pan. Way-shower."

Moc'Tor thought a moment before answering. "Way-shower. For some reason, it strikes me as the perfect name. But then she comes from the perfect mate. I could not love you more, E'ranale. How you have stood beside me through all this."

She placed her hand alongside his face and stroked his cheek with her thumb. After a moment of silence, she asked, "Moc'Tor, do you really think the Others do not know we have been taking their seed?"

"I cannot say, E'ranale. On the one hand, it seems they must know something is going on. Maybe they do not want to admit any knowledge for fear of causing a direct confrontation. It is perhaps, as the females said, that the dreams are pleasant, but as a forbidden aberration in their pleasure practices, the males are reluctant to share them. It is possible there is no group disclosure. After all, we have taken what we needed as peacefully as possible, doing them no harm. They know we could easily overpower them if we wished, although it is perhaps an unspoken understanding. But then again, there is nothing about the dream that gives us away as the source."

"Since you gave the females the right to refuse a male, how easily we have set aside one of our most sacred tenets; Never Without Consent," sighed E'ranale. "I do not believe we are quite at the end of this path yet, but we do need to remember everything we have learned so far—that which is truly important."

"I am not following."

"Laws, Moc'Tor. I think the High Council needs to establish laws that we can all agree on. Laws that will direct and guide us in the future."

"That is a good idea, and I agree with you. I will present it to Straf'Tor and the other council members. If we can come to a consensus, such laws could unite all our communities."

The High Council had grown out of the original band of Leaders, back when Moc'Tor first proposed cross-breeding with the Others. He had become the official Overseer, and the group met regularly to get updates on the progress that Lor Onida and Oragur were making with the other communities. Kthama Minor served as the central location of Lor Onida and Oragur's work.

Lor Onida and Oragur had since paired and were living at Kthama Minor. Deeper inside the system, the inner walls of the largest chamber were covered with markings. These represented the original pure Mothoc males and females, along with the chart of their pairings and offling—either offling with mates of their own communities or with those born of the Others' seed. When the Others' seed had been introduced, the Mothoc decided to trace the genetic line through the females until that line started breeding true and the Other's seed was no longer required. This, however temporary, bothered a fair number of the males, who resented that more and more power continued to be granted to the females.

Straf'Tor had stood up to address the Council. "A suggestion has been made to set down agreements, standards of behaviors—laws if you would—to guide our fellow communities and us as we move forward into this new age."

"Give us an example, Straf'Tor," a female from the crowd asked.

"I am not talking about restrictions that go against our general nature. I am talking about statements with which we can all readily agree. Such as never commit violence against another except in self-defense. Or that the needs of the community come before those of the individual."

"Or—never without consent?" added a sarcastic male voice.

Straf'Tor had known that was coming. Much of the rising strife had to do with the very practice that had saved them from extinction. "Your point, Garl'-Tar, has been made often. Move on."

"My point needs to be made again, Straf'Tor. There are many of us who agree with it, and you are one of them. This has gone far enough. We have achieved our objective, and we must cease this abomination against the Others. We agreed to it in the beginning because it was the only way to avoid the complete dying-off of our people. But our population is re-established. There is no need to continue. Already, the next generation looks more like the Others than the Mothoc. Where will it end? When no part of the Mothoc is left at all?"

In the background, voices joined in to support Garl'Tar.

"And what of our culture?" he persisted. "The genetic lines used to be traced through the males but are now traced through the females. The balance of power was off in the beginning, it is true. We males treated the females as if they were ours to mate with as we wished. But that has all changed. We corrected our error only to go too far in the other direction. The females have too much power now!"

Even more voices, louder ones, joined that of Garl'Tar.

Straf'Tor did agree with Garl'Tar. The cross-breeding had gone almost dangerously far and certainly far enough—but that was not the point of the assembly, and he had to bring it back on track.

"That is not the subject of this meeting. We came here to agree on guidelines, standards of conduct. We all recognize there are strong feelings on both sides, but for now, can we not put them away so we can at least accomplish this goal?"

After the mumbling had quieted down, the group agreed that there should be at least three laws for the community at large; The Needs of the Community Come Before the Needs of the Individual, Honor the Females in all Matters, Show Forbearance for the Failings of Others.

The second statement had been hard-won, but Straf'Tor and Moc'Tor argued strongly for it. They did not want to forget the sins of the past, especially with the resentment now brewing against the females. In the face of this growing sentiment, there was a need for a statement lifting the females, not pushing them back down. Neither would budge, and the Council members all stayed into the late hours before Moc'Tor was finally able to dismiss them.

Straf'Tor had returned to his quarters where he could consult Ushca and enjoy some solitude with her. "There was dissension again in the Council meeting over how far to continue using the Others' seed. There is a large group that feels we need to stop where we are. What do the females think about this?"

"I do not know what they think in other communities, but here, most of them wish to continue. The females are now used to their appearance, and with each generation, they see the benefit to the offling increasing. The younger generations are now more inventive, faster, and have finer muscle control. They are not as strong, but they are still far stronger than the Others. Like us, they will have few natural enemies."

"Has Lor Onida told you anything at all about the other communities?"

"Yes," she sighed. "There is something that fits directly with your concern, Straf'Tor. The People of the Far High Hills are rumored to have taken it further. Several of their females produced offling from Waschini seed."

Straf'Tor stopped cold and stared at his mate. "Waschini? Are those not the rumored pale, fragile versions of the Others who are said to have come across the icy waters in huge floating shelters? How is that possible? I thought they were a myth. They do exist?"

"That is how the story goes, yes. Some females came across what seems to have been several sentries on foot. They were far separated from any others. The females were attracted to their startling hair coloring, almost the color of the sun."

"I do not believe it. I am not convinced they are

even real. I would have to see one. Did they bear offling?"

"From what I was told, yes. For some reason, they are even smaller than any of our other combinations produced. They have very little overall body covering. And what they do have is very light—almost the color of the winter wheat. They will have to take after the Others in wearing wrappings. But the mothers were already several generations modified."

"I need to confirm with Lor Onida how true this is. If it is accurate, then it is time. The line must be drawn, and it must be drawn hard. It is one thing to do what we have to do to survive; it is another to spit in the face of the Great Spirit by taking matters too far. After having come this far in recovery, if this is not stopped, it will bring destruction upon us all, and on Etera."

The next morning, Straf'Tor requested the presence of Lor Onida and Oragur. Before long they stood before him, and Straf'Tor had his answer. He was enraged. The females of the Far High Hills had indeed stolen seed from the Waschini and produced offling. The Waschini had not survived the encounter.

Straf'Tor stormed across the room, his arms stretched wide. Lor Onida, Oragur, and Moc'Tor watched him in silence.

"Is this what we have become? Is this who we are now? Is it not bad enough that our females use their abilities to subdue the Others, sneak into their villages, and take what they want from them? Have we forgotten they are our wards whom we are supposed to be protecting? Oh yes—I know that no harm is done if you do not consider performing such an intimate violation on another as harming them. The fact that it is females doing this to males should make no difference. Oh—but now it has gone further. Now they have killed to get what they want."

Moc'Tor stepped forward. "Straf'Tor, that is not true. They did not kill the Waschini—at least not intentionally."

Straf'Tor continued, unfazed. "We have no fear of the Waschini. The stray washed-out ones that are said to come across the waters are no threat to us. But it is of no benefit that they become aware of our existence. It may be better that they were frightened to death—or whatever caused them to die. But that does not change the fact that this abomination has to stop. And you heard Lor Onida.

"There is even more to the story," continued Straf'Tor. "The females were far, far out of their territory. There is no explanation, no excuse for what they did. They should be punished, but as far as I know, their Leader, Tres'Sar," he pointed at Lor Onida, "your Leader, looked the other way. Enough. Enough."

Moc'Tor reminded them that he had said words

to that effect many years ago. He had said enough over another instance where an act had almost been committed without consent—the young maiden of the Others, whom Trestle, the impaired young male, had intended to violate. He was one of the first born with problems, the specter of things to come. Now, again, they were arguing about the same issue—imposing one's will on another. "To him, it was a drive, no different than eating when hungry or drinking from the stream when thirsty. Luckily, the maiden survived the trauma. So I gave his mother a choice—we could either kill her son or crush his seed pack, permanently removing his mating drive."

Moc'Tor still struggled to get the image out of his head of how Oragur had carried out the act, though after Trestle recovered, he was gentle and quiet and never caused any trouble again.

"We must come to an agreement, brother," said Straf'Tor. "We must stop this before it goes any further. Say you agree with me, and together we can put an end to this."

Moc'Tor slowly shook his head. "I wish I could, Straf, but I cannot. It seems we are at an impasse. You have a following that wants to stop where we are. My people want to continue because we see the benefit of the Others' seed line mixed with ours. We intend to move forward another generation to make sure we continue to breed true. Perhaps then we will stop."

"Perhaps then? So you admit you see no end to this?"

"I am not saying either; we will decide according to my people's wishes. This is not something I alone can dictate."

Straf'Tor glared. "Is it not? Decades ago, did you not give a speech stating exactly that? That it is our place as Leaders to do exactly that? And were you not just now talking about laws and standards of conduct? For the love of the Great Spirit, if this is not where we should be setting limits, then what is?"

"Straf'Tor, our father has been gone for some time now. It is just you and me; we must lead together."

"And yet you are the one making it impossible. How can we lead together when we are divided on this critical aspect?"

"It is late. Perhaps we should stop and calm down," said Moc'Tor.

"We can stop, brother. But nothing will change tomorrow. Or the next day. Or the day after. If you have made up your mind, if you will not stop this abomination, then there can be no peace between us. I can no longer stand here and condone what you are doing."

"What are you saying, Straf'Tor? Are you talking about war?"

Straf'Tor scoffed. "It would be a short war, Moc'-Tor. Your followers are frail compared to mine. They are stronger than the Others, but there is no comparison with us in strength. You may think your offling are more inventive, but that matters little when our offling can, at will, snap any of yours like a twig. They disgust me!"

"If our community splits, Straf, we are the largest. It will divide all the other communities. Is that what you want?"

"I never wanted that. But if it has to be this way, then so be it. You are ignoring our obligation to the Great Spirit to provide for Etera. I am appalled that you, the Guardian, would do so. Even you, brother, will not live forever. Yes, there is your daughter, Pan, but she is not well-enough versed in the Order of Functions, and we can all see the strain this division is having on you."

"Do not lecture me on the importance of the Order of Functions. And do not bring my offling into this. When it is time for her to take her place as Guardian, she will be ready. You speak of the strain caused by division, yet it is you who support that division. And how can you support division when it goes against everything we believe?"

Straf'Tor started to walk away but paused for a moment, his back to his brother. Hardly turning his head, he said, "We will stay until the laws are agreed upon, and then we will leave Kthama. There are fewer of us than of you; it is only fair that we are the ones to leave. I am sorry it has come to this, but this is where we are. And once we leave, there can be no contact between our people ever again. If it has fallen to us to serve Etera alone, then so be it. But I will risk no more contamination of my people with your thinking."

Moc'Tor watched his brother walk away. His heart was heavy, and he was more tired than he remembered ever being. He walked the corridors aimlessly until he found himself outside Kthama.

The Guardian looked up at the canopy of stars. What had he done? But what other choice had the Great Spirit given him? There was no other choice; it was this or perish. But was it still what the Great Spirit truly wanted? Had Moc'Tor taken his community too far down that path? He could not believe they were wrong. *Our offling are far more advanced than we are. The future belongs to them. Why can Straf and the others not see that?*

Moc'Tor felt he had failed in some way; had he failed his people? They could not afford a rift, but neither could Moc'Tor prevent one. Straf'Tor was right. *Our offling's ingenuity is no match for their offling's size and strength.*

If Moc'Tor could not change their minds, then he must allow this division because in a battle between the two branches of offling, without a doubt, Straf'-Tor's following would be the victors. And as Straf'Tor had stated, what of the Mothoc blood? In the rush to find a solution, maybe Moc'Tor had not given that enough consideration. In a flash, the realization hit him. Straf'Tor was right; the Mothoc blood must not perish from Etera.

Moc'Tor bent over, resting his hands on his

knees. I, of everyone, should have kept this need at the forefront of my decisions. How had he lost his way? Perhaps he was indeed no longer fit to lead.

He would give Straf'Tor time to calm down and then talk to him again.

I will try one more time. If he still wants to take his band of followers and leave, then I will concede. I could not stop them, anyway. But at least they had set out their laws first. Perhaps if they could achieve that much, they could maintain peace—some form of unity in spirit.

Moc'Tor returned to Kthama to seek relief and a few moments of peace in the arms of E'ranale but found her curled up on their mat, already asleep. However, he needed to talk to her.

"E'ranale, are you awake?" he asked. She stirred a bit but did not reply.

"E'ranale, are you awake?" This time he touched her shoulder.

She sleepily turned to him, thinking, Well, I am now. "What is it, Moc'Tor? Is everything alright?" She brushed the hair from her forehead.

"I am worried, E'ranale. I have been so focused on ensuring our survival that I forgot our first duty to Etera. Straf'Tor is right—we cannot breed so far with the Others that the Aezaitera is compromised. Whatever happens next, we must keep the two seed lines separate. For the protection of our offling and for the continuation of what is left of our Mothoc blood. I fear I have taken it too far already."

"What are you planning to do?" she asked.

The next morning Moc'Tor sought out his brother.

"We need to talk."

"What would be the point? We said everything last night."

"I have given much thought to your words. And I have come to realize you are right. We cannot allow the Mothoc blood to be diluted much further. But there is room on Etera for us all, and the division between us, which I have seen as a loss, I now see as necessary protection of the different paths we are taking. I am truly humbled at the wisdom in the Order of Functions—that which you have rightfully accused me of abandoning, but which directs us without our conscious awareness."

Moc'Tor paused a moment in reverie.

"I am calling the original Adik'Tars together," he continued, "those who are still alive from when we started down this path. I believe there is a bigger plan of which we were unaware—something more complex than a disagreement between two brothers. We are the largest population, and what we do will affect the other communities as well."

"I am glad you have come to your senses. What are you thinking?" asked Straf'Tor.

"I have a plan," said Moc'Tor, "but it will take both of us, and perhaps others, to make it happen. I have already sent sentries out with word to assemble, and I expect that within several days we will have enough Leaders to meet. I hope Lor Onida will be able to attend. I have lost track of how far along her seeding is. She is an integral part of what has happened and can answer any questions."

"I agree that we need her there. I believe she has some time yet before she delivers."

"I will find out how Lor Onida is doing. I can send for Oragur or that female who is often with her, Irisa. Let me know when the Leaders start to arrive. But first—"

Straf'Tor listened as his brother laid out what he proposed they do.

Within days, there were enough of the original Leaders, including Lor Onida, for them to go ahead with the meeting.

Moc'Tor looked out at the circle of familiar faces. Hatos'Mok of the Deep Valley; Tres'Sar from Lor Onida's community, the Far High Hills; Tarris'Kahn from the small group up the river—even Solok'Tar had made it from the Great Pines. Not everyone had come, but it was enough. Moc'Tor, E'ranale, Straf'-Tor, Toniss, and Oragur brought the number to ten.

As Overseer, Moc'Tor spoke first. "Fellow Adik'-Tars, I will get straight to the point. The path laid out before us for our survival, the path we all agreed to take, has now become a source of division. For many generations, we have used the seed of the Others to provide offling. As we all know, the longer we continue this practice, the greater the physical changes. But not just size; there are changes in physical abilities too. Some of us see these as positive, and others see them as negative. That is part of our division

"My brother and I are on opposite sides of the matter. Our father died some time back, and I find it particularly hard that the only solution we can see will end up dividing forever what is left of my family. No matter—it is clear that a great division is about to come. But before that takes place, it is my hope that we can agree on a set of laws to collectively follow as the basis of our culture, so though our physical differences will increase, our foundational ones will not.

"If we agree that we cannot agree and the division has to go ahead, let us at least have laws on which we can agree."

No one said a word. The silence told Moc'Tor everything he needed to know. He stepped down, and to start the discussion, joined the others at the table.

Accepting that the division might take place somehow helped them focus on what they needed to do. Before the day's end, they had agreed on the rest of the laws.

1. The needs of the community come before the need of any one individual
2. Honor females and do not subjugate them
3. Show humble forbearance for the failings of others
4. No hand may be raised against another except for protection or defense
5. In conflict, use the least amount of force necessary
6. Protect, heal, and shelter the sick, helpless, and those in need
7. Offling are our future and are sacred
8. Never take more than you need
9. All contact with Outsiders is forbidden
10. Never without consent

These were declared the Sacred Laws and would be made known to everyone. Lor Onida recorded the laws as clearly as she could in symbols on a piece of hide for later transfer to the great wall of Kthama Minor. Memories were short, and she was a believer in records, as was her mate, Oragur.

Despite the progress made, a pall hung over the group when they disbanded for the evening. As hard as that day had been, the next day they would start the even more painful discussion of division and exodus from Kthama.

CHAPTER 11

Straf'Tor could not sleep. The next day's events were weighing on his mind. He was glad that Moc'Tor had come to his senses about their role in Etera. He was prepared to take his followers and leave—he had been for some time. But he knew that once they left, they would never return. Everyone and everything at Kthama would be lost to them forever. The other communities were also divided. He imagined only several dozen would come with him. Even the other 'Tor siblings were divided. Some would go with him, and some would stay at Kthama with Moc'Tor. But at least he had some peace now since they both realized that the division was necessary, perhaps even part of a greater plan of which neither could conceive.

Morning found him still lying there, going over and over what was to come.

All the Mothoc Leaders, the Adik'Tars, were assembled. Once they had agreed on the details, they would address the entire population of the High Rocks.

As usual, Moc'Tor opened. "Let us make this as thorough as it needs to be, but as brief as possible. Straf'Tor, tell us your plans."

"Since we cannot agree on the collective future of our people, my family, my followers, and I will vacate Kthama. We will be leaving as soon as we can. The Leaders who are in support of continuing to interbreed with the Others, are you willing to release those within your communities who would join with us instead?" Straf'Tor looked around the group, unsure who was of the same mind as him.

"I support our current path, but any of my people who wish to join you certainly may do so," said Hatos'Mok of the Deep Valley.

"I think we all would agree to that, Straf'Tor," said Solok'Tar.

"I agree, too," said Tres'Sar of the Far High Hills.

"That surprises me, Tres'Sar," sneered Straf'Tor.

"Why would that surprise you, Straf'Tor? I do not wish to hold anyone against their will."

"Oh, but you will allow your females to suck the male seed from the unconscious bodies of the Waschini without their consent! That is an interesting set of standards you have there. Who knows what matter of abomination your females are producing up there now!"

Tres'Sar had finally had enough of Straf'Tor's insults and leaped across, knocking him against the wall. "Who do you think you are, Straf'Tor? Do you think you are above this? You agreed in the beginning that it was our only way. Would you rather we had all died out by now? Because that was our only choice!"

"I did agree!" shouted Straf'Tor, breaking away and spinning around to pull Tres'Sar's hands behind his back. "But we are past that point. We have done what we had to do, and there was no need to take it this far. We have shamed ourselves. You and my brother have shamed us by bringing us into this age of darkness. Look at your offling. They barely resemble us any longer. They practically shiver in the halls of Kthama. Their modesty is hardly covered. In some cases, their skin is not even as dark as the Others. And all are so pale compared to ours—like the creatures that scramble in the deepest levels of Kthama, deprived of light too long. Is this your legacy to our future? Each generation becoming weaker and frailer? And what of the Aezaitera? Krellshar!"

The others stayed back, letting the two enraged warriors burn off their anger. They were well matched; it was unlikely that one would do irreparable harm to the other before they drained each other's reserves.

Tres'Sar struggled and broke one hand free from

Straf'Tor's grip, spinning around in turn and slamming his free fist directly into Straf'Tor's jaw. Straf'Tor released Tres'Sar's other hand, which Tres'Sar then brought around, landing an uppercut to the bottom of Straf'Tor's chin, snapping his head back.

Both males were thrown apart in opposite directions and collapsed, bent over on the floor, catching their breath.

Straf'Tor rose, his hand nursing his chin as he locked a bone-chilling stare on Tres'Sar. Tres'Sar pulled himself to his feet and circled, looking for an advantage.

"You do not want to continue with this, fine," Tres'Sar said. "But do not tell us what we can or cannot do. You lead your people; I will lead mine, as will the other Leaders. But do not come crawling back to us when, five generations down the road, you are back to where we were before, with grieving mothers cradling deadborn offspring and imbeciles who do not know any better than raping their sisters."

"Enough!" shouted Moc'Tor stepping between the two males. "Enough! Nothing good is being accomplished. You are not listening, Tres'Sar. There are two paths open to us. No, we do not agree, but we can at least part on good terms instead of creating this bitterness and division between us."

"It is too late for that, Moc'Tor," said Tres'Sar. "Bring your message to my people, Straf'Tor. Anyone who wants to is welcome to leave with you. But once you have had your say and collected your following —if any—they may never again return to the Far High Hills."

Though they were not part of the inner council meeting, by now, guards had entered the room and stood ready to intervene at Moc'Tor's command.

Moc'Tor addressed them, "Your services will not be needed; this is nothing more than a friendly dispute between family members."

The guards stood down but remained against the wall.

Having had his final say, Tres'Sar spat at Straf'-Tor's feet and stalked to the back of the room.

Moc'Tor turned to those remaining.

"Nothing more will be accomplished here. Tres'Sar is right. The best we can do is go our separate ways as soon as possible. Make your arrangements, Straf'Tor, and let me know when you will be leaving. I will address the people of Kthama this afternoon."

With that, almost all the others dispersed to their respective corners of Kthama.

Almost all.

The room fell silent—more silent than seemed naturally possible. Quiet and still under the weight of the heavy mantle carried on the shoulders of those who remained. They had decided. Enough. It had fallen to them to bring the end to Wrak-Wavara, the Age of Darkness, and to protect the future of Etera.

After a moment of reverence, Moc'Tor's voice broke the quiet. "Now, we wait. Once the division is complete, we will put an end to Wrak-Wavara."

CHAPTER 12

Decades passed, then centuries. As memories faded, but before lessons learned were lost, the time had come for the final piece to be put in place. What had needed to be done was done. But now, the time was right.

At the appointed time, in the secret depths of Kthama Minor, the selected Leaders came together to take the final step on the journey of leading their people through the Wrak-Wavara.

In the quiet sanctity of the night, into the mind of every Akassa and Sassen on Etera—a Connection opened. More powerful than had ever been experienced by any of them.

Each one found him or herself pulled into a darkness bleaker than could be imagined. In total silence, a light slowly dawned, just bright enough to reveal a circle of dark-haired, faceless bodies. Though they were legion, they spoke in one voice.

To each Sassen, they said, "We are Mothoc. We are keepers of Etera; our blood and the Aezaitera are one. What had to be done was done. But no more. Never again, the Wrak-Wavara. This is Rah-hora. Sassen, make no contact with Akassa lest you yourselves are destroyed. Leave the Others to them. We leave you to the future of your own making. When the Wrak-Ayya falls, the Age of Shadows, the true test will begin. We will be watching."

For each of the Akassa, the People, they had a different message— "We are Mothoc. We are keepers of the Others. What had to be done was done. But no more. Never again the Wrak-Wavara. The Others who are our wards are now your Brothers. Learn their language. Make amends. Regain their trust. Leader to next Leader—Kthama Healer to next Kthama Healer—only these may speak of this past. This is Rah-hora. We leave you to the future of your own making. When the Wrak-Ayya falls, the Age of Shadows, the true test will begin. We will be watching."

And then, just as those in the inner circle had opened the Connection, so they closed it.

Before they parted, Moc'Tor uttered the last words ever to be spoken in Kthama Minor.

"Kah-Sol 'Rin." It is done.

Change came hard to the People, but in the end, it was change that saved them.

○

The People seldom spoke of what they had each dreamed, and then only in the most hushed of circles. It might even have been dismissed and forgotten forever, except for the undeniable physical evidence that it all had been real. The massive stone that none but the Mothoc could have put in place, forever sealing off Kthama Minor and the shameful history of the Age of Darkness.

The People honored the Rah-hora. They began the process of repairing their relationship with the Brothers. The location of Khama was cloaked by the Mothoc, erased from Sassen knowledge for the protection of the Akassa.

In time, with dirt and vines covered the carving, and the entrance was forgotten—except among the Healers of the High Rocks, who passed the story down from one to another, each before their death. To all other communities, Kthama Minor, and the truth of their true history disappeared from memory.

○

The Akassa did not replace the Sassen. The Akassa and Sassen walked together with the Fathers for many generations. Then there were two branches; The Akassa, the

Sassen. And the Fathers-Of-Us-All created the First Laws while the two communities were still intact. Is that why we seem to share them with the Sarnonn? Khon'Tor could not stop thinking about Haan's statements. He still struggled with the fact that they'd had the history wrong, all this time. *And what is the contract Haan keeps mentioning?*

During a short break, Khon'Tor, Acaraho, Adia, Nadiwani, and Tehya stayed to speak directly with the Overseer.

Acaraho spoke first. "From what Haan just told us, we share the First Laws. I would like to know what their First Laws are, to see just how closely they fit. Time has a way of changing things. If we share the law about No Contact With Outsiders, that still does not explain the nervousness of the male Haan sent to us earlier—his messenger."

"For every answer we get, we get five more questions," said Khon'Tor. "When we restart, we need to get to the heart of why we are here. We hoped to find other tribes, and more communities of our own people, but so far, other than Haan's community, we have not made contact with any others. And based on what he says about their avoiding contact, had he not had a life-threatening need for the Healer's help, I doubt we would even now know they exist."

"I suspect that Haan's problem is similar to our own," said Adia.

They looked at each other but said nothing.

Tehya broke the silence. "I assume that you think Haan is going to ask us to breed with them?"

There it is, thought Khon'Tor. *How she can be so quiet most of the time and then speak her mind like that, I will never understand. It needed to be said. Oh, little mate, you are braver than the rest of us.*

"I believe he will," said Acaraho.

"What is the problem?" asked Tehya.

Acaraho and Khon'Tor looked at each other. "You want to answer that?" Acaraho asked.

"You go right ahead," said Khon'Tor.

Acaraho cleared his throat. "I do not want to appear shallow; however, the idea of mating a Sarnonn is not an attractive thought. I doubt we would get any volunteers."

"I doubt that the Mothoc physically mated with the Brothers. The size difference alone makes it implausible. Surely if we find the Sassen unattractive, the Brothers would find the Mothoc doubly so. I imagine that however they accomplished it before, is how it would be accomplished now. Only perhaps we could solicit their permission this time instead of doing it without their consent," Tehya finished.

Kurak'Kahn smiled at the wisdom in Tehya's simple, common-sense answers. The more he was around her, the more he understood why Khon'Tor cherished her so.

"There are considerations other than the mechanics of it. Mixing our bloodline with theirs; is that a direction in which we want to go?" asked

Kurak'Kahn. "Who among you saw Hakani's offspring by Haan?"

"I did. She definitely had characteristics of both tribes," answered Adia. "But just because we help them does not mean we cannot pursue our own path for our females."

"It is one thing for our males and Haan's females to agree, but when it comes to our problem, there is no way to get consent," said Acaraho.

Kurak'Kahn sighed heavily. "No matter how we look at it, we are back at Wrak-Wavara. Since we do not believe we can mix with the Brothers again, that leaves only the Waschini. And the Waschini can never know we exist."

"But who would volunteer to—" Khon'Tor said.

"If things were to change, and there was a way," said Nadiwani, "I would volunteer to be seeded by the Waschini. I believe others would too, for the sake of the People."

"Whichever path we take, Overseer, we need the help of your record keepers," Adia said.

"Yuma'qia and Bidzel, yes," said Kurak'Kahn. "Let us hear Haan out, and later we can continue this conversation about our path with the other council members."

As the others trickled back into the room, Adia was lost in thought. *Is this why I rescued him? Is this the purpose for which Oh'Dar was brought to us? To somehow help us connect with and interbreed with the Waschini? If so, this is something only he can do. Perhaps he is the bridge between our two tribes. Khon'Tor claimed that his being an Outsider was a problem, and yet it may, after all, prove to be part of a solution we did not even know we needed.*

"Settle in, please. Haan, it is getting late. May we ask how we can help you?" asked the Overseer.

"My people are solitary. After the Sassen left Kthama, we returned to the old ways of mating. No more restrictions of one male to one female. This was a bad decision for the Sassen, but Straf-Tor, the Sassen Leader, and his followers resented the Akassa ways. Now, because of this error and isolation, we are in the same situation as before. No new males, no new females. We need new seed, the same as the Fathers did in the ancient times. Otherwise, our offling will suffer. Your scouts will find no other Sassen, or Sarnonn, as you call us."

"We would not have found you had you not approached our sentry," said Khon'Tor.

"The Laws still hold. Sassen will only approach Sassen."

"Your Laws, you mentioned them before, Haan. You said we share the same Laws. Tell us what your laws are," Khon'Tor said.

"Needs of the family come before the needs of the one, females are to be honored and never set below males, remember your own failings when blaming others, inflict no harm unless defending yourself, win with least amount of force necessary, shelter and protect the sick and helpless, offling are the root of the future, do not be greedy, no contact with the Akassa."

Acaraho, Khon'Tor, and Adia all looked at each other.

"No contact with the Akassa? Not anyone else, specifically us?"

"Contact between the Akassa and the Sassen has been forbidden since the time of Wrak-Wavara when our paths separated. Your ancestors stayed here at Kthama. Mine left to live at Kayerm. Since then, we have kept the contract and concealed our existence. Kthama's location was unknown to us—concealed. Only when we tracked one of your sentries back did I learn where to find Kthama."

"You have spoken of a contract more than once, Haan."

"Yes. From the time of Wrak-Wavara. It was the only way to save your kind."

Heads turned to each other.

"Save us from what?" asked Kurak'Kahn, the High Council Overseer.

"From *us*."

A cold pall fell over the room as Haan's words

shattered all built-up reassurances of the Sarnonn's goodwill toward the People.

"Haan—" was all Adia could get out.

And then as if to make his point, Haan stood.

The walls of Kthama had always seemed generous to the People. The caverns were naturally large, but some of the corridors and tunnels had intentionally been widened. Chisel marks worn by age were still visible enough to betray that they had been enlarged well beyond their original size. Many doorways, ledges, and ceilings grossly exceeded the levels and allowances needed for the People.

All eyes followed Haan to his full height when he rose. Even at that, there was still ample clearance above his head to the ceiling of the meeting room. Whether Haan meant it as a demonstration or not, the point of the Sarnonn's unmatchable size and strength did not go unnoticed.

Then the smallest of all the People, Khon'Tor's mate, Tehya, rose and padded over to Haan. Khon'-Tor's blood ran cold as he watched his beloved, delicate female approach the mountain of the seemingly unstoppable power that was Haan. "You mean us no harm. You said so yourself."

Haan bent over and picked up the delicate Akassa female, hoisting her up near his shoulder, where she wrapped her arms around his neck as far as she could. Haan's massive flesh-ripping canines were inches from Khon'Tor's vulnerable, irreplaceable female.

Acaraho reached over and pressed his hand down hard on Khon'Tor's shoulder and felt a tremor pass through the Leader's steel frame. Khon'Tor had never felt so helpless or so terrified in his life.

Haan carried Tehya over and gently placed her down next to Khon'Tor, who was using every shard of his iron will to contain his instinct to attack the Sarnonn.

Once on the ground, Tehya moved closer to Khon'Tor. She looked at him when she realized he was shaking. Even though his mate had been returned safely to him, Khon'Tor kept his eyes locked on Haan.

Haan turned back to address the High Council.

"My people mean no direct harm to your people. But by making contact, I have broken the contract, the agreement between our people and the Fathers-Of-Us-All."

The hair was standing straight up on the back of Kurak'Kahn's neck, but he stepped closer to Haan, regardless.

"The Fathers? Haan, you said the Mothoc are the Fathers-Of-Us-All. *But what contract? What agreement?*" His fear and frustration showed in his voice.

"The Sassen were never to make contact with the Akassa. The Mothoc feared the Akassa would lead the Sassen in the wrong direction, convincing us to follow your ways. The Fathers wanted the Sassen to stay more—what is the word—*pure.* Too much of

Mothoc was already lost, even in the Sassen. On the other side, you are weak, defenseless against us. The Sassen were to stay away from you for your protection as well. Should the Sassen contact the Akassa, the contract would be broken."

"*What contract,* Haan?" Kurak'Kahn repeated the question.

"The Rah-hora."

Acaraho and Khon'Tor looked at each other.

The Sarnonn had a Rah-hora with the Mothoc to avoid the People. That is why the messenger Haan sent was so afraid of us; he knew he was breaking the Rah-hora. But Haan and his people would not fear the Rah-hora unless— Kurak'Kahn's mind was silently racing.

"Are the Mothoc still alive, Haan? They must be, for you to fear breaking the Rah-hora."

Haan did not answer Kurak'Kahn's question, but continued, "The Mothoc also made a Rah-hora with the Akassa—never to repeat Wrak-Wavara. The records were hidden, the Rah-hora and the location of the Wall of Records is known only to Healers of the High Rocks."

Slowly, as if on cue, all heads turned to look at Adia, who sat with her mouth open.

CHAPTER 13

Adia pulled herself together and stood to address the High Council Overseer, who was staring at her along with the others. "I promise you, Overseer, and the rest of the council, I know nothing of a Rah-hora nor any of this information that Haan has shared."

Khon'Tor rose to speak. "Overseer, they are both speaking the truth. Remember that our former Healer suddenly died—before Adia came to join us. If the information was passed from Healer to Healer at Kthama, then it died with her."

"Then you do not know of the Rah-hora. Or The Wall of Records at Kthama Minor?" asked Haan.

Adia's head was spinning. *It is too much. Extinction, a Rah-hora with the Fathers of the past—and a wall. A wall where?*

"Haan, how is it you know so much about

Kthama, and what happened here? Can you tell us that?" asked the Overseer.

"What is done is done. I have broken the Rah-hora. It is time that the Akassa know as much as I can tell you. Since the Healer knows nothing about Kthama Minor and the Wall of Records, when I return, I will show you. There is too much to explain."

"When you return, Haan?" asked Kurak'Kahn.

"Yes. This is a serious matter. I must prepare myself and my people if we are to open Kthama Minor."

Silence in the room.

"Haan, the High Council needs to discuss this without your presence. Do you understand? Khon'Tor will find you later before you leave," said Kurak'Kahn.

"Yes. I will go and find Akar and tell him we are going home soon."

Khon'Tor spoke, "With your permission, I will allow Akar to stay. He seems to have his mind set on it."

Haan let out a formidable sigh. "He is like his mother. Hard to turn once his mind is set on a path. Always hard to manage. It is your decision, Leader of the People of High Rocks. He is of age, and he is of your blood."

Khon'Tor nodded, and with a sigh, Haan left to find Akar'Tor.

Kurak'Kahn stood to address the room.

"What Haan has shared has shaken many of our earlier beliefs. It is a lot to take in. We do not have time to waste. We must decide if we are to help Haan and his people. If we do not, we may lose his favor; however, we have to look at each decision on its own merits—not as a bargaining tool for what he knows. Who would like to speak first?"

Risik'Tar of the Great Pines rose. "The matter of the Rah-hora raises great concern. Haan intentionally broke it by coming to Kthama. That means either the stakes are as high as the risk, or he does not believe the Mothoc still exist to enforce it. Whatever this Kthama Minor and the Wall of Records is, it sounds like it is critical to our path forward. I believe we need Haan's knowledge, but as far as helping Haan goes, that does not change our path at all. Though there may be a problem getting volunteers."

Silence.

"Whatever methods they used during the Age of Darkness may still be available to us now. Surely our culture has advanced further than theirs. If it worked for them, it should work for us. And in this situation, there would be consent on both sides, as far as helping Haan is concerned," added Risik'Tar.

Lesharo'Mok was next to stand. "I see no reason for this Haan to mislead us in any way. If their plans were to conquer us and take back Kthama, whatever resistance we could offer would soon be overcome. Ultimately, they would win. There is no need for deception or our consent. They can take whatever they want—including our males or our females."

"Of anyone here, other than Acaraho, I have had the most interaction with Haan," Khon'Tor said. "I agree with Lesharo'Mok. Haan is looking for our cooperation and help. I believe we should give it to him. We can work out the details later, but clearly, we will need volunteers, regardless of how it will happen."

"Healer of the High Rocks, what do you say?" asked Kurak'Kahn.

"We know that it would require our males and their females because our females cannot carry a Sarnonn seed to term. Based on what I know of Haan, I agree with Khon'Tor. We should help them. It does not harm us in any way. And the key to this may lie in whatever Kthama Minor is." Adia looked at Urilla Wuti, who simply nodded her agreement, as did the other Healers in attendance.

The Overseer spoke up. "Are we in agreement then? We will help Haan's people if we can? Let us put this to a vote. Are we willing to help Haan's people?"

Each person in the room either stood as a sign of agreement or remained seated to dissent. For almost the first time in the Overseer's rule, everyone was standing together in agreement.

"It is decided then. We will help Haan. As far as

our own path goes, after much consideration, it appears the only way open to us is with the Waschini. Let us end this meeting now and reconvene when Haan is ready to open Kthama Minor."

With that, the High Council meeting was called to a close, with a plan for those who could return to do so later

Haan found Akar'Tor. "I am leaving soon. Are you coming with me?"

"No, Father, I hope not to. I am going to ask Khon'Tor one more time if I can stay. If he again refuses, then I will return to Kayerm."

"You are needed at Kayerm. Your place is with us, but you must discover that for yourself, I am afraid," said Haan.

"I have no place there, Father. Maybe in your eyes, but what is my future there? There are no females who will have me. I am not strong enough to lead Kayerm. In time you will take a second mate and produce more offling, and one of them will take over. But it will never be me, and we know that. The only place I am not an Outsider is among the Akassa."

"Then find another Akassa community, Akar. There is nothing for you here but trouble."

"I do not agree, Father. Everything I want is here."

Haan shook his head.

Just as they were finishing, Khon'Tor stepped into the room. "Haan, the High Council has unanimously decided that we will help you. However we can," said Khon'Tor.

"Thank you. I will prepare for the next step and return later. I do not know when."

Khon'Tor turned to Akar'Tor. "If your father agrees, I have decided that you may stay. But my hospitality stands only as long as you follow orders. You asked to learn about our ways; your training will start tomorrow morning. After the morning meal, report to me."

Khon'Tor then turned to Haan. "When are you leaving?"

"Tonight. I am anxious to see my mate and our offling."

"Safe travels, Haan. Until you return." They shared the reverent Sarnonn gesture of brotherhood, and Khon'Tor left the room without giving Akar'Tor a second glance.

Hakani looked up from nursing to see her mate standing in the entrance of their living space, holding back the skin curtain.

"I am glad to see you return, my mate. Is Akar with you?"

"He is staying at Kthama, for now."

"Khon'Tor is letting him stay?"

"Yes. But Akar has some difficult lessons ahead of him."

"Is the High Council going to help our people, Haan?"

"Yes. But I need to address our people first, as I need their help."

"And what are Akar's plans? Is he looking to find a mate there?"

"I think his interest in Kthama goes further than mating, Hakani. Prepare yourself that he may never return. Focus on your daughter."

Then Haan knelt before her with a sigh. "We must not mate again, Hakani. The Healer made me see that it was wrong of me, and you could have died because of it. You may select another female for my needs. But you will retain your role as my First Choice."

Hakani nodded. Instead of being jealous, she was relieved. *Thank the Great Spirit. I do not think I could get through that again.* Her mind went immediately to Haaka as a second mate for Haan. She and Haaka were already friends, and she thought she had caught the female looking Haan over when Hakani appeared not to be paying attention.

And as far as Akar is concerned, perhaps he will be successful in insinuating himself with the People. Then, even if it takes a year to make a place for himself, maybe I can return to Kthama. If I then reveal what Khon'Tor did to Adia and me, the uproar might force him to step down. And who would be the rightful heir then, but Akar'Tor!

The next morning, Akar'Tor found Khon'Tor seated with Acaraho, Adia, and Tehya in the eating area.

"I have come as you asked, Khon'Tor."

Khon'Tor did not look up to acknowledge Akar'Tor but kept eating. "First of all, I did not ask you to find me; I ordered you to. That is an important distinction and one you need to learn fast. Now, you are to find Mapiya, one of the Leaders of the females. She will probably be in the food preparation area. She will tell you what to do."

"A female? What can a female teach me?"

Khon'Tor stood then, and stared at Akar'Tor. Despite their similarities, Khon'Tor's countenance broadcast loud and clear that he was a Leader and a force to be reckoned with. Akar'Tor, standing next to him, though virtually a physical duplicate, seemed more like an adolescent than a grown Akassa.

"First of all, your question tells me you have even more to learn than I feared. Secondly, what were you expecting?" Khon'Tor baited him.

"I am your son. I would expect to learn how to lead, how to fight—all the things that make a Leader. And to know when you will make the announcement about my taking over from you in the future."

"I will lay down a path for you, but I will not clear

the way. You must do the work yourself. As for an announcement? I will make no such announcement. This is an opportunity, Akar; that is all I am giving you. What you do with it determines whether there is any chance for you ever to live among the People. You must earn the right. I will not grant it to you undeserved and unproven, just because I made a mistake in who I mated."

Akar'Tor turned red and looked at the others at the table, careful to avoid looking at Tehya, then turned and stomped off. Khon'Tor's glare followed him hotly.

Akar'Tor fumed silently. *I will make you pay. And after you are out of the way, I will take your mate Tehya for my own! I will lead the People, and I will be a greater Leader than you ever were!*

Everyone at the table was thinking the same thing. *This is going to get a lot worse before it is over.*

PLEASE READ

Dear Readers,

You have made it through Book Six. I am humbled by your continued interest in my writing. Hopefully there is something you are liking (or loving maybe even, she says hopefully) the series.

It takes months and months to write a book and get it through the review, editing, and publication process. The production costs to produce a book (cover design, editing) can easily run over $1K a book. Writing a book or a series is a labor of love in hopes of pleasing you, the reader. It requires charts and tables of plot lines, character attributes, vocabulary lists, and ideas for twists and turns which may or may not get incorporated.

All authors dream of creating the next hugely successful story. Of course, it happens to very few; but we get tremendous pleasure out of knowing that you enjoyed our work and were entertained by it. So, if you enjoyed this book, and the others before, I would very much appreciate your leaving a positive rating. If you know of others who might enjoy the series please let them know.

To leave a review on Amazon, return to your Orders page and click on Digital Orders. Next to the book cover should be a link to "Write a product review". Even if you only leave a star rating and do not feel inspired to write an actual review, I would greatly appreciate it. Positive ratings on Goodreads are also appreciated!

If you would like to be notified when other book in this series are available, you can follow me on Amazon - or if you would like to join the mailing list, please subscribe to my newsletter here:

https://www.subscribepage.com/theeterachroniclessubscribe

The next book in the series is Book Seven: The Edge of the Age.

ACKNOWLEDGMENTS

I want to thank all of you, my readers.
You have made this effort worthwhile.

Made in the USA
Las Vegas, NV
09 February 2024

85513257R00177